He was in a deep well...

One of the men got up, walked to where Barrabas lay motionless and kicked him in the back of the head.

"Enough!" Joshua shouted. "I don't want him badly injured."

The man looked sullen, then cheered up. "My brother..." he started to say.

Joshua ignored him and leaned over to pick up Barrabas's P-38. "You and your brother were useless," he remarked with a sneer.

"We must be paid!" the man said with some urgency.

"You will be," Joshua replied, and shot him.

The woman came over to join Joshua and stood looking down at Barrabas with a puzzled look on her beautiful face.

"Take a good look at him, my dear," Joshua said, smiling. "He too will get what's coming to him."

SOLDIERS OF BARRABAS

SOLDIERS OF BARRABAS

THE BARRABAS HIT

JACK HILD

A GOLD EAGLE BOOK FROM
WORLDWIDE.

TORONTO · NEW YORK · LONDON · PARIS
AMSTERDAM · STOCKHOLM · HAMBURG
ATHENS · MILAN · TOKYO · SYDNEY

First edition March 1989

ISBN 0-373-61629-5

Special thanks and acknowledgment to
Joe Roberts for his contribution to this work.

PROLOGUE

Central Africa, 1986

Barrabas was eating dirt.

All the SOBs were on their bellies as bullets whined and whizzed over their heads. It was an ambush.

"Christ," O'Toole said. He was lying closest to Barrabas. "They were waiting for us."

"Maybe not for us," Barrabas said. "Maybe for just anybody."

"Yeah, but they got us."

"Not yet they didn't," Barrabas said. That was when he got up on his knees and squeezed the trigger of the AK-47 he was holding.

"Jesus," O'Toole said, and he crawled next to his leader and began to fire his own weapon.

Soon all the SOBs were up. Billy Two started the rush forward, a war cry on his lips. Terrified, Philip M'Basa's troops scattered as if they had seen a ghost— or a Hawk Spirit.

"I don't know who's crazier," Liam O'Toole told Nile Barrabas later, "you or that loony Indian."

"He's crazier," Barrabas said. "I've got audacity."

With the enemy temporarily dispersed, the SOBs continued their trek through the jungle. Their aim was to find Thomas Gilkenny and his team of mercs and hook up with them for an assault on M'Basa's ammo dump.

It had been Walker Jessup who got Barrabas and his SOBs into Central Africa to fight Philip M'Basa's attempted takeover of a small African country that was currently being run by Oliver Besant. Besant was what Jessup called a "friendly," whereas M'Basa would be virtually impossible for the United States to deal with. It was common knowledge that M'Basa's whole operation had been financed by the Soviets, although no one came right out and admitted it.

Thomas Gilkenny and his men had been hired by Besant himself. The arrival of the SOBs had taken Besant by surprise. He hadn't asked for any American help, official or unofficial.

"I have my own soldiers, gentlemen," he had said to Barrabas, the SOB commander.

"We're mercenaries, Mr. President," Barrabas had explained.

Besant had smiled, white teeth flashing from a very black face. "I have my own mercenaries. Why should I need any more?"

But in the end Besant needed all the help he could get. Using Soviet funds, M'Basa had armed his men with the finest guns money could buy, weapons that were much superior to those wielded by Besant's men.

What M'Basa's men did not have was competent leadership. M'Basa himself was a politician, not a soldier. He would have done better to hire Thomas Gilkenny—before Besant did. In the end, Barrabas knew, it would be Gilkenny who would make the difference—Gilkenny and the SOBs together.

Barrabas had served with Gilkenny in Vietnam, and knew him to be a master tactician. A little headstrong, but a master, nevertheless. By demonstrating his talents and exercising his strong will, Gilkenny had established himself as an "unofficial" general in Besant's army.

Now the SOBs were following directions they'd received secondhand from Gilkenny. They were to join him in an assault on M'Basa's supply base—where he kept his weapons, his ammo, his gasoline, everything he needed to make his army move.

But the ambush had slowed them down so much O'Toole was concerned. "It'll be a disaster if Gilkenny goes in without us, Colonel," he said, "but I'm afraid that's what he'll do. He hasn't got the patience to wait."

"He'll wait," Barrabas said, but, with O'Toole, he knew his words expressed only wishful thinking. His soldier's instinct told him Gilkenny would not wait.

THOMAS GILKENNY couldn't wait.

"We're going in," he said to Bill Marlowe, his second in command.

"Shouldn't we wait for Barrabas and his men for cover?"

"We don't need Barrabas. We'll leave Besant's men behind for cover," Gilkenny explained.

"But that leaves just us—" Marlowe began.

"We're dealing with a bunch of monkeys with guns, Marlowe," Gilkenny interrupted. "How many of us do you think it takes to handle them?"

"Us" was just eight men, Gilkenny's personal merc force.

When Barrabas and his SOBs had arrived Gilkenny had not been pleased. He knew Barrabas's team was a first-class fighting force—they had to be, with Nile Barrabas leading them—but he was convinced his team was better. Hell. He knew *he* was better than Barrabas, though he'd never had a chance to prove it—especially not in Nam, where Barrabas had outranked him.

Now he had a chance to prove his superiority.

"Let's move," he told Marlowe. "Tell the jigs they're providing cover, then follow me."

The SOBs heard the firing as they approached the clearing, and Barrabas looked at O'Toole.

"I told you he wouldn't wait," O'Toole said.

"Shit," Barrabas said.

When they reached the clearing their suspicion was confirmed. Besant's men had been left behind to provide cover, while Gilkenny and his men had gone into M'Basa's camp alone.

"We'll go in after him," he shouted to O'Toole. "Tell Besant's men to keep providing cover."

O'Toole nodded and relayed the message, then joined the other SOBs as they followed Gilkenny and his men into the rebel camp.

M'Basa's rebels had been taken by surprise by the attack, and had had to scramble for their weapons. Many of them were naked, or clad only in underwear, as they returned the fire Besant's men were laying down.

Once he and his men were inside the rebel camp, Gilkenny sent Marlowe and three others to take care of M'Basa's weapons-and-explosives tent. With it gone, the rebels would soon run out of ammo and would be unable to fight back. He took the other three men and headed for the gasoline tanks. With their fuel gone, M'Basa's men wouldn't be able to hunt them down, then.

Gilkenny had no respect for Besant's men, always referring to them as monkeys with uniforms. He did have respect for Besant, though—and his money. After all, the man had been smart enough to hire Gilkenny!

As he and his men approached the fuel tanks Gilkenny was cursing Barrabas. The colonel and his men were supposed to be there laying down covering fire. Though he was reluctant to admit it even to himself, he'd have felt safer with cover from Barrabas than from Besant's men. But so far everything was going fine.

So far.

Once M'Basa's men recovered from the surprise, armed themselves and pinpointed the location of the covering fire, they were able to concentrate their return fire. Some of them managed to work their way close to where Besant's force was. Besant's men started to feel the heat, and did what untrained troops always do when they can't stand that heat. They abandoned the kitchen!

"LISTEN!" O'TOOLE GOT Barrabas's attention. "No more cover fire."

"Shit," Barrabas said. "Besant's men have been broken."

"What now, Colonel?" Nanos asked. "Pretty soon we're going to be the central attraction."

They were inside the camp now, where M'Basa's men would soon be returning in force.

Before Barrabas could answer, there was a tremendous explosion, and they all turned their heads to look.

"Ammo," Claude Hayes said.

"That's half the job," Lee Hatton shouted.

"Let's see about the other half," Barrabas said. "The gasoline."

As they charged forward, suddenly gunfire broke out behind them. M'Basa's men were returning to the camp. The exploding ammo tent had distracted some, but others were firing at Barrabas and the SOBs, assuming they were responsible for the explosion.

"Return fire!" Barrabas shouted.

He wondered where Gilkenny was, and hoped he was about to destroy the gasoline tanks. As events had turned out, Barrabas and the SOBs were distracting the rebel forces as planned; the only difference was they were doing it from inside.

Some isolated explosions still came from the ammo tent—or where the ammo tent had once been—as explosives continued to be triggered, but a big blow—like gasoline—was needed to cause enough confusion for the two mercenary teams to withdraw.

"Billy," Barrabas shouted to the SOB nearest him. "Come with me."

"Right, Colonel."

Barrabas caught O'Toole's eye. The Irishman knew what the colonel was about to do. He and Billy Two were going to find the tanks.

Barrabas ran, Billy Two's huge presence a comfort beside him. If indeed Billy Two's Osage Hawk Spirit came to him at times like this, it was nice to have the two of them along.

Then Barrabas saw Gilkenny, standing next to a stack of gas containers, shouting orders at his men. Some of them were obviously wounded—bloodstained and staggering. They were being fired on. Barrabas and

BillyTwo laid down some fire of their own, trying to get M'Basa's forces off Gilkenny and his men.

For a split second Barrabas's eye caught Gilkenny's. The other man shouted something that Barrabas couldn't hear.

He wasn't sure he wanted to hear it.

What Gilkenny had shouted was, "Where the hell were you!" But he knew the SOB leader couldn't hear him.

Gilkenny was well aware by now that he had made a mistake in not waiting for the SOBs. Barrabas and his men would not have broken and run the way Besant's had, and consequently would have kept M'Basa's soldiers distracted for a longer period. Gilkenny's mercs would not have become pinned down the way they had been. Only now, with Barrabas and his men in camp, were they getting a short reprieve.

Gilkenny called out to his man, Curtis, who was carrying the explosives they would use to get rid of the fuel. "Here! This way!"

Curtis turned and nodded, continuing to fire but backing up as he did so. Finally he turned, and he and Gilkenny ran to the containers of gasoline.

"Get it set," Gilkenny instructed Curtis.

On his knees, Curtis started to place plastic explosives among the containers, just as the ground in front of Gilkenny was suddenly chewed up by bullets. Gilkenny returned the fire.

M'Basa's soldier raised an AR70, aiming at Gilkenny, but before the merc leader could turn to face him the gunner fired. It all seemed to happen in slow motion. As the enemy's bullet struck one of the gas containers the thought, *Grenade bullet!* flashed through Gilkenny's mind. Then the gasoline went up.

The explosion was tremendous, lighting the sky with yellow-and-orange flame. The force of the blast knocked Barrabas and Billy Two to the ground. From his prone position Barrabas saw a man on fire. It could only be Gilkenny.

"Jesus!" he said as the man ran. He got to his knees and raised his AK-47. He intended to fire at Gilkenny and put him out of his misery, but before he could do so Billy Two pushed him down, saving his life as several chunks of hot lead passed through the space where his head had been.

Billy two returned fire and the other SOBs rallied as Barrabas looked into the jungle. The running man had left a burning trail behind him, and Barrabas wished he could have helped him.

He hoped the man didn't live to suffer too much longer.

Ablaze, the man ran through the jungle, screaming and beating at his body with his burning hands. As he ran he prayed for death. And suddenly there was no ground beneath him. He had run right off a ledge. His legs churned in the air as he fell, he hoped, to his death.

As he hit the cold water his last lucid thought was, God, don't let me live through this!

But he did.

1

Nile Barrabas went out on the balcony. He was naked, but the hotel suite was high enough that there was little chance anyone could see him. If someone did, and didn't like what they saw—well, too bad.

In the bedroom behind him Erika Dykstra had just fallen asleep. A peaceful sleep was not something that came easily to either of them. Pleased that she had at last fallen into a deep slumber, he didn't want to do anything to disturb her. She would have felt the same way had the tables been turned.

Below him sprawled Athens, Greece, a city at peace at this late hour. He could see Constitution Square—called Syntagma by the Greeks—and across the square the Tomb of the Unknown Soldier. These were big tourist attractions, well lit at this time of night. In the distance he could see in silhouette the famous ruins of the Acropolis.

He had brought Erika to Athens so they could both rest and get away for a while from the violence that pervaded their lives—Barrabas's life more than Erika's, though violence had more than once spilled over from his life into hers. On a few occasions it had almost gotten her killed, and at least once it had stigmatized her. That she had recovered so well from all that was a testament to her strength.

It was also why he loved her.

The cool breeze was refreshing as it played over his skin, drying a light film of sweat. A tall man, he stretched to his full height, reaching as high as he could with his hands. His soldier's body was well muscled and graceful, covered with the scars of his profession, and his hair was prematurely white.

He stood on the balcony for a long time. Then the breeze suddenly felt cold, and he went inside.

Still naked, he sat in an easy chair, half reclining, with legs stretched out in front of him. He didn't want to wake up Erika by getting into bed with her. Over the years he'd developed the ability to sleep sitting up, if he had to.

But sleep did not come easily for him this night. His eyes were still open when the phone rang. Its sound was a soft hum rather than a harsh ring, but he pounced on it anyway, lifting the receiver before Erika could be disturbed.

"Hello?" he said, wondering who would be calling him there. Even the Fixer, Walker Jessup, had said Barrabas needed this time away from things. Jessup would only bother him if it was an extreme emergency, a matter of life, death and national security.

Wasn't it always?

But the voice that came to him over the line was not Jessup's.

"Colonel?"

It was a woman's voice, and he had to strain to hear it, as if it was being muffled by something.

"Hello," he said again, "Who's this?"

"Colonel," she repeated, then more stridently, "Nile!"

Suddenly he thought he recognized the speaker. "Lee? Lee Hatton?"

"Colonel...I...I'm in trouble....Ohhh!"

The last seemed to be a cry of pain, and he sat straight in the chair. "Lee, what is it? Where are you?"

There was a moment of silence, then the sound of static. He thought they'd been cut off, but then he heard her voice again, faint and full of pain. "They say they're taking me to the Acropolis," she said. "To die."

"Lee? Lee!"

This time, after the static, came silence. He was sure they had been cut off. He hung up the phone and hurriedly got dressed.

He considered waking Erika, but decided to leave her a note telling her of Hatton's call. If he wasn't back by the time she woke up, she would know what to do. He scribbled the brief note quickly, glanced at his watch and added the time of his departure to the message.

The last thing he picked up before leaving the room was his P-38. Even on R & R the weapon never left his side. Such was the nature of his business, and his life.

AMONG THE PILLARS of the mighty Acropolis the man called Joshua waited. The woman was standing out in the open, where she could be seen by the light of the moon. Her skin was dark and her dark hair covered half her face.

Two other men were also behind the pillars, lackeys hired by Joshua for this night's work.

Joshua smiled, satisfaction glowing inside him. Finally, months of planning were about to give way to the perfect execution of his purposes—to a perfect execution of his enemy.

BARRABAS SAW LEE HATTON, standing in the moonlight. Or was it her? He squinted his eyes. In the darkness it looked like her.

"Lee? Is that you?"

"Nile?" she said.

"Lee..." He took a step forward.

He heard the footfall behind him and turned swiftly, to parry the blow with his forearm and hit his attacker in the face with his fist. The man staggered back. Another took his place, charging at Barrabas. Barrabas sidestepped, and the second attacker went sprawling onto the ground.

The other man was up and running at him again. This time Barrabas raised one leg and kicked out hard with all the force he could muster. The heel of his shoe smashed into the man's jaw, and he went down.

Barrabas drew the P-38 before either attacker could get up, and backed away a little so he could cover both of them.

"All right," he said, "up." He heard movement behind him. "Lee?"

Something crashed into the back of Barrabas's skull, and suddenly the moon was gone and he was falling into darkness.

One of the men on the ground got up, walked to Barrabas and kicked him in the back of the head.

"Enough!" Joshua shouted. "I said I didn't want him badly injured."

The other man staggered to his feet. He tried to speak, but could make no intelligible sounds. Joshua guessed that Barrabas had broken the man's jaw.

"My brother—" the first man started, but Joshua cut him off.

"Your brother and you were useless," he said as he leaned over and picked up Barrabas's P-38.

"We must be paid!" the first man said.

"You will be," Joshua said, and shot them both.

The woman came over and stood next to him, looking down at Barrabas.

"Take a good look at him, my dear." With his foot Joshua turned Barrabas onto his back, and a shaft of moonlight fell across the colonel's face.

"Capturing him was the object of this exercise," Joshua said, "and yet . . . it is just the beginning."

ERIKA WOKE TO A SHAFT of sunlight that cut across the bed and hit her right in the eyes. She lifted her arm to ward it off, then turned over to escape it completely. It was then that she discovered Barrabas was not in bed with her.

"Nile?" she called, sitting up. When she got no answer she threw back the sheet and swung her legs over the side of the bed. Again she called, "Nile! Are you here?"

A tall blond woman with a sleek body that was full and firm, Erika stood and padded naked across the bedroom, to look in the living room of the suite. She knew Barrabas would have left a note. There it was, by the phone. She wondered if he had gone out for breakfast, not wanting to wake her, but somehow she didn't think he had. She had a nagging feeling that something was wrong.

She picked up the note and read it.

Erika,
Got a call from Hatton. In trouble—0410 hours.

Nile

Short and to the point. Lee Hatton was in trouble, and had called at 4:10 a.m. Nile had gone to help her and hadn't bothered to wake Erika.

Erika liked Lee Hatton. In fact, Lee had been immeasurably helpful to her after her terrifying experience with Karl Heiss. She hoped Lee's "trouble" wasn't serious, although she realized it couldn't have been a trivial matter or Lee would not have called Barrabas in the middle of the night. There was something else about Lee's call that bothered Erika, but she couldn't put her finger on what it was.

Erika called room service to order brunch, and by the time she showered and dressed, her food had arrived, along with an English-language newspaper. She took her time reading the paper, but the thought of Lee in trouble kept nagging at her. She put down the newspaper and looked again at Nile's note. He's been gone a long time, she thought.

That was when she finally realized what it was about Lee's call that hadn't seemed right. What was Lee doing in Greece? Erika had thought she was enjoying some peace and solitude at her home in Majorca. Had she called Barrabas from Majorca? No, for if he had gone there to help her he would have packed a suitcase and would certainly have left a more detailed note, or woken

Erika to tell her where he was going and why, and to say goodbye.

Erika looked in her address book for Lee's phone number, and with the assistance of the hotel operator she placed a call to Majorca.

After the sixth ring, she was on the point of hanging up when someone answered the phone.

"Hello?"

"Lee?" Erika asked. She suddenly felt very cold.

"Erika? Is that you?" Lee said. "I thought you and Nile were going to Greece."

"We are in Greece."

"Then why are you calling?" Hatton's voice suddenly became guarded. "What's wrong?"

"I—I don't know, Lee. I woke up a couple of hours ago and found Nile was gone."

"Maybe he went out for a walk—"

"He left a note."

"What's it say?"

"Lee, he says you called him about four o'clock this morning and said you were in trouble."

"*I* called him?"

"Yes."

"And he went out?"

"To help you, yes," Erika said. Her heart was pounding. "Lee, something is very wrong."

"Just sit tight, Erika," Hatton said. "We're on our way."

Lee Hatton hung up the phone and took a moment to compose herself. It wasn't she who had called Nile Barrabas, but someone had, and had convinced the SOB leader that it was she.

It was obvious that Barrabas was in trouble.

She thought a moment, then picked up the phone and dialed a number in Washington, D.C.

It was time to call the Fixer.

IN WASHINGTON Walker Jessup was on his way out of his office when the phone rang. He was tempted to keep on walking, because he was on his way to an early lunch. Walker Jessup seldom let anything interfere with his meals. This time, though, something made him answer the phone.

"Mr. Jessup?"

He recognized the voice immediately. The fact that Lee Hatton was calling him could only mean trouble.

"What is it, Hatton? What's wrong?"

She told him about the call from Erika Dykstra and their belief that something had happened to Nile Barrabas.

"Nile has never had any trouble taking care of himself, Lee."

"Mr. Walker, someone called him pretending to be me in trouble, and now he's missing. He's been gone about twelve hours. I'm going over there."

"All right, all right," Jessup said, "you'll need the rest of the team. Do you know where they are?"

"Billy Two and Nanos are in Oklahoma. Billy wanted to show Alex some sacred Indian rite, or something."

"Can they be reached by phone there?"

"No."

The fat man sighed. "Can you get in touch with the others?"

"Yes."

"All right," he said, "I'll take care of contacting Billy and Alex. And Lee?"

"Yes?"

"I'll come myself, as well."

"Thank you, sir."

Jessup hung up, then picked up the phone again to arrange for the small private plane he had occasion to use from time to time. He hoped lunch would be served during the flight to Oklahoma.

LIAM O'TOOLE WAS SITTING at a small desk in his New York apartment, rewriting a section of the screenplay he was working on. For some time now O'Toole had been trying to have a film made featuring his poetry, and he had finally decided to go ahead and write his own screenplay.

When the phone rang he ignored it until it jangled the fourth time. He picked it up and said, "Sorry I can't answer your call right now. At the sound of the beep leave a message—or just hang the fuck up!"

He was about to imitate the beep of a real answering machine, when his caller cried, "Liam! Don't hang up!" It was Lee Hatton's voice, and she sounded strident and on edge.

"Lee?"

"Is Claude with you?"

"He's here in New York with me, but he's out right now." Claude Hayes was the only black in the SOBs, just as Lee Hatton was the only woman. Often, when they were between assignments, O'Toole and Hayes hung out together.

"What's wrong, Lee?"

"We're needed in Greece, Liam."

"What's in Greece?"

"Nile, and he's in trouble."

"What kind of trouble?" O'Toole asked, becoming instantly and totally alert.

"He's missing, Liam."

He put his pen down and said, "Where do we meet?"

ALEX NANOS KNEW he was going to die.

He could feel it in his burning lungs, in his pounding head, in his aching feet and knees. Shit, even his balls hurt!

Ahead of him ran William Starfoot II, known as Billy Two to his fellow SOBs. His huge strides ate up the ground effortlessly. Nanos knew that Billy's lungs weren't burning, his head wasn't pounding, his feet and knees and balls weren't hurting.

"A hundred-mile run through sacred ground will open you up to the gods," Billy Two had told him. "They will enter your soul and purge you of your impure and vile thoughts. I am doing this because you are my friend, Alex."

Some friend, Nanos thought, forcing me to run a hundred miles just so I won't have nasty thoughts anymore. On top of that, Billy had made him wear moccasins. Every stone he stepped on had left a dent and a bruise that he'd probably bear for life! And the sun! It was beating down on his head and back, so hot that he would have sworn his skin must be burned black by now.

Staring at the back of his huge Osage friend, Alex Nanos was having some of the nastiest thoughts of his life.

He was looking around for some kind of escape route when he became aware of a vehicle approaching. It was a four-wheeler, and in the passenger seat was one of the fattest men he'd ever seen.

"Jessup!" he said, coming to a halt. Billy Two ran on, apparently oblivious to everything around him. Nanos wondered why the fat man had tracked them down out here. He moved to intercept the jeep, which braked to a halt in a wild cloud of dust.

"Thank God you're here!" Nanos said, grabbing Jessup's pudgy hand.

Jessup, surprised, pulled his hand away abruptly. "What's gotten into you?"

"You've come to take me away from here," Nanos said. "Bless you."

"Get hold of yourself, Nanos!" Jessup told him. "We have a long trip ahead of us."

"Where are we going?"

"Greece."

"Oh, thank you, Lord!" Nanos the Greek said, looking skyward. "What's in Greece, beside my heart?"

"Barrabas is," Jessup said. "And he's in trouble."

Nanos's demeanor immediately became serious and attentive. "What's wrong?"

"He's missing, Alex. He's disappeared."

Nanos climbed into the jeep. "Catch up to Billy," he instructed.

Jessup slapped the driver on the shoulder and the man urged the jeep forward, stirring up a new cloud of dust. As they moved up alongside of Billy, Nanos jumped out and grabbed the Osage's arm. The driver stopped the jeep, and he and Jessup watched with interest as Nanos pulled Billy Two to a halt.

"What are you doing?" Billy Two demanded, pulling his arm away. "You can't interrupt the sacred run of—"

"The colonel's in trouble, Billy," Nanos said. "He needs us."

Immediately Billy Two stopped struggling, and moved toward the jeep. "We're wasting time," he said.

He reached the jeep well ahead of Nanos, who climbed in after him. When Jessup lumbered back and got in, his driver took off in a cloud of sand and dust, heading for the small plane he had recently landed in the desert.

As BARRABAS CAME TO he thought he could smell the ocean. He opened his eyes. He was lying on his side, and should have been staring at the wall, but all he could see was a wall of black. For a moment he thought he was blind, then he realized he was blindfolded. He tried to reach for the blindfold with his hands, but they were bound behind his back. He pulled at his bonds for a few moments, then stopped to rest.

Frowning, he tried to recall what had happened after he left the hotel. He knew he had gone to the Acropolis. By day it was crawling with tourists, but at night it was just a collection of huge shapes and oblong shadows. He had seen a woman who looked like Lee. He had been on the point of asking her what was the matter, when something had come out from behind one of those shadowy shapes and hit him on the head.

He thought of Lee now. Was she all right? Had it even been her on the phone? More than likely he had been duped. The more he thought about the static on the phone the more he realized that its purpose had been to cover up any differences he might otherwise have noticed between the voice on the phone and Lee's. The woman at the Acropolis had said only one word, and he hadn't been close enough to see her clearly.

He lay still now and concentrated on finding out as much about his environment as was possible while he was tied and blindfolded.

His hands told him that he was lying on wood, possibly a floor or some kind of bunk. His nose told him that the ocean was near. In fact, the slight roll he felt indicated that he might be at sea. Perhaps he was on the bunk of a boat cabin.

That would mean he was being transported away from Athens, but if so, where was he being taken? By whom? And why?

The short note he had left for Erika in his haste to rescue Lee Hatton had not said where he was going. How would anyone ever find him?

WHEN WALKER JESSUP, Alex Nanos and Billy Two entered the suite that Erika Dykstra and Nile Barrabas had shared, Lee Hatton, Claude Hayes and Liam O'Toole were already present.

"What have we got, Lee?" Jessup asked, as soon as brief greetings had been exchanged. The question was directed to Hatton because it was she who had put out the call for the team to assemble, and he assumed she had arrived in Athens before any of the others.

"Not much," she said. "Erika woke up shortly after noon yesterday and found Nile gone. He had left her this note, which doesn't say where he went."

Jessup took the note and read it, then put it in his pocket. "Such a foolhardy move on Barrabas's part wasn't like him," Jessup said.

"We were just saying the same thing when you walked in," Liam O'Toole responded.

"And I had just said that it was not necessarily true," Lee Hatton said.

"Explain, doctor." Jessup settled his bulk in a chair and tried to ignore the rumbling of his stomach.

"I think Nile was concerned for me, obviously, but also concerned not to put Erika in any danger. If he had awakened her she might have insisted on going along. I think he simply decided to avoid that confrontation. And, to argue about it would have taken time. And perhaps he was afraid that if he said where he was going, she would follow him there."

Jessup thought a moment, then said, "Your argument has merit, doctor."

"Thank you."

"Well," Jessup said, addressing everyone in the room, "how do you suggest we proceed?"

Liam O'Toole was the first to answer. "Let's get down to the basics. Wherever it was he went, he obviously was not able to return."

"Then we assume he's been taken," Claude Hayes stated bluntly.

"I think we have to," Nanos agreed, and the others nodded.

"But by who?" Billy Two asked.

"That's what we're all here to find out," the Fixer said.

"Then I guess we'd better get to it." O'Toole got to his feet. "Separately we can cover a lot of ground, and by tonight we should know if anyone saw him leave the hotel.''

The others rose also, but Jessup called for them to stop a moment. "I think you should coordinate your movements with Nanos," he suggested. "This is, after all, his home turf."

Alex Nanos had spent his formative years in a Greek fishing village, not in the nation's capital, but he did not argue the point with Jessup. The fact was that he did know Athens better than any of the others.

As the SOBs left, having agreed to report back in two hours, Erika Dykstra said to Jessup, "And what am I to do? Just sit here?"

"No, my dear," he replied, "you can call room service and order in some food."

"Food?"

"When the others return," Jessup explained, "they'll be hungry. Order up some cold cuts and things, some coffee, beer, perhaps some wine, and ask them to bring it up in two hours. And for now, perhaps you can order something for you and me to eat right away."

"I'm not hungry."

"Order something anyway. You and I are going to talk, but I don't want you overextending yourself."

"Talk about what?"

"About what you might have seen or heard since your arrival here in Athens."

"I haven't seen or heard anything that would help—"

"Perhaps you have and you don't know it," Jessup interrupted her. "That's why you will tell me every move you and Nile have made since your arrival, and you won't think about it too long or hard. Just let it come, and I'll do all the thinking. If there's something there that will help, we'll have to root it out."

"Oh, all right," she said.

"But first," he reminded her, "take care of room service."

The fact of the matter was, he'd be able to concentrate much better once he had something in his stomach, and their conversation over the next two hours was going to take a lot of concentration.

2

Barrabas was helpless—gagged, blindfolded and tied to a chair. He did not know how he had got from the bunk—or the boat—where he had first regained consciousness, to this chair. He had been taken to the toilet by someone who had also been on the boat, someone who had not spoken a word. No food or drink had been offered to him during his captivity. The position was painful and was probably the reason he'd woken up. He was also hungry and thirsty.

His hands were bound behind him and his feet were tied individually to the legs of the chair. He could tell that the wooden chair was sturdy enough to withstand his attempts to shatter it by overturning it. He would simply have to wait until whoever had captured him was ready to talk to him.

If and when that time ever came.

One floor up from the cellarlike room where Nile Barrabas was incarcerated, the man who had captured him sat listening to a report from a subordinate.

"Are you sure they're all in Athens?" he asked when the man had completed his report.

"Oh, yes, sir," the other man said. "They are all there."

The man stole a glance at the woman in the room. She had dark hair and was very tall. Her breasts were small, but perfectly formed, and highly visible because of the bikini she was wearing.

"Even the fat man?"

"Yes, sir, even the fat man."

The bikini was black and skimpy. The woman's hips were slender, but her buttocks were rounded and firm. Her legs were long and sleek.

The man reporting was named Stanley Wolenski, a small-timer from New York City who had transplanted himself to Greece. Wolenski was small in stature, but even if he'd been bigger he would have been intimidated by the man he was talking to.

He did not know who the man was. He had been instructed to address him as Joshua. He was sure that was not the man's real name, but as long as Wolenski was being paid the sums of money he was, he was perfectly willing to call the man anything he wanted to be called.

Wolenski noticed that Joshua looked pleased with the news he had brought, especially the part about the fat man. He wondered what the fat man and the others—and the man in the cellar—meant to Joshua, but he didn't ask. It wasn't his business.

He waited now to hear what further instructions Joshua had for him. During the pause he eyed the woman again. She was sitting by the window, which was open, her face lifted to the sun. She had a lovely profile, but he couldn't take his eyes off her body.

"How many men do you have?" Joshua asked, jarring the man back to the business at hand.

"Enough."

Joshua glared and repeated. "How many?"

"Seven."

"Are they... competent?"

"They're the best."

"Then I want every one of those people watched."

"They will be," Wolenski said. "They won't even know my men are there."

"Wrong. I want them to know your men are there."

"What?" Wolenski asked. He pulled his eyes away from the woman again, not sure that he had heard correctly.

"I want them to know they're being watched, being followed."

"Is that wise?" Wolenski asked.

"Whether it is wise or not is of no consequence, nor is it your concern," Joshua returned. "It's what I want. Are you being paid enough to give me what I want, Mr. Wolenski?"

"Oh, yes, sir," Wolenski said, "more than enough."

"Then do as I say."

"What are my men supposed to do once they're spotted?" Wolenski asked.

"They are to wait."

"For what?"

"For further instructions."

Wolenski took a last look at the woman then, just long enough to notice that her smooth olive flesh was tanned even darker. He moved toward the door, trying to recall the woman's name, which he had once overheard. Was it Julie? No... Julia? Close, but not quite. Well, it would come—

"There'll be no need for you to come back here again, Mr. Wolenski. You will make your future reports, and get your future instructions, by radio."

"Yes, sir."

"Payment will be deposited in your bank, as before."

"Yes, sir. Thank you."

After Wolenski left, Joshua stood up from his chair and walked to the woman sitting by the window. He put his hand on her taut belly, enjoying the smoothness and warmth of her skin.

"He's a wretched little man," she said.

"I know."

"His eyes offend me, crawling over my body like that."

"I know," Joshua said again. "But perhaps he would rather look at you than at this." He pointed to his face, which was more than half covered with shiny scar tissue.

The woman, whose name was Julianne, reached out and touched the ruined face tenderly. She never even opened her eyes.

"He's a fool," she said, seeing him with her hand. "You are beautiful."

"*You* are beautiful," Joshua said.

Julianne smiled. "I know."

They were both right. The woman's beauty was stunning. She had long, straight black hair, dark eyebrows, olive skin and brown eyes shaped like a cat's.

The man, except for the scar tissue, was an Adonis. His body, had been undamaged by whatever had ruined his handsome face, and remained smooth and well muscled, though not muscle-bound.

"When this is over, will you kill him for me?" she asked.

"Unless you wish to do it yourself."

She thought a moment, cocking her head to one side, then said, "No. I think watching you do it will be enough."

"As you wish."

He leaned over and kissed her, breathing in her seductive scent. She did not move at all, except for her mouth, which returned the kiss, and her tongue, which darted into his mouth.

"I'm going to work on my tan," she said. She reached behind her, causing her breasts to jut out, and released the bikini top. It fluttered to the floor, revealing firm breasts as brown as the rest of her body. Her erect nipples were even browner than the rest of her.

He bent his head and kissed each of her nipples, then pulled the strings on either side of the bikini bottom. She raised her hips from the chair so that he could slide it away from her. The hair between her legs was dark and curly. He then removed the skimpy bathing trunks that were his only garment.

Sliding his hand down over her belly to the dark curly hair between her legs, he said, "You can work on your tan later."

She reached her hand out and took hold of his hardness. "Yes," she said.

BARRABAS THOUGHT he could hear voices upstairs. He'd gotten to the point where he was certain he was in a cellar, but he could still faintly smell the sea. Perhaps he'd been taken to one of the many Greek islands.

He remembered reading somewhere that the islands of Greece numbered more than fourteen hundred, but that only about one hundred and sixty were inhabited. He could be on one of the Ionian islands, the Sporades or the Cyclades, or anywhere in the Aegean sea; the Dodecanese were possible, or, of course, Crete, which held the labyrinth where the legendary Minotaur had lurked. Corfu was the largest and most popular to tourists of the Ionian Islands. On Skíros, of the Sporades, Odysseus discovered Achilles, whose mother had hidden him there, disguised as a girl, at the beginning of the Trojan Wars. Delos, one of the Cyclades, was the birthplace of Apollo, the god of the sun.

Barrabas suddenly realized his mind was wandering, bringing forth details about the Greek islands he hadn't realized he knew. For the first time he became aware that his head hurt, in the back. He didn't remember being hit but knew he must have been. He wondered how hard the blow had been. Was his mind rambling because he had a concussion? That might account for how heavily he'd been sleeping since his capture—not even being aroused when his captors moved from the boat to wherever he was now.

He had to concentrate, try to keep his mind on the straight and narrow.

He was sure now that he could hear the drone of voices upstairs, but could not make out what they were saying. There were the deep but differing tones of two men, and then suddenly there seemed to be only one, still intermittent, though, as if he was talking to someone else, someone Barrabas couldn't hear. Either a softer-spoken man or a woman.

Moments later he heard a woman cry out. It was not a cry of pain, but of pure, unadulterated pleasure.

And there were more to come.

"I'M TIRED," Erika said.

"I know." Jessup nodded. "So am I."

Erika passed her hand over her forehead. "Where are the others?"

Jessup checked his watch and replied, "They should be here soon. Is this room air-conditioned?"

"I'll turn it up," she said.

Jessup's shirt had huge, wet rings around his underarms, and he suspected that he smelled. He had little to do with women, but suddenly he was aware of not wanting to offend Erika.

"I'm going to go to my room and take a shower," he said when she returned from adjusting the air conditioning. He got up and picked up his jacket from the back of the chair.

"You could shower here," she offered.

Momentarily at a loss for words he mumbled something about all his clothes being in his room, and thanked her anyway.

"It should be cooler in here when you come back," she said as he walked to the door.

"Good. If the others return tell them I won't be long."

"All right."

"And check on that spread from room service, will you?"

She looked at what was left of their dinner—his plates as clean as if they had been licked, hers with much of the food still untouched. "Sure," she said.

Erika called room service to make sure the meal she had ordered would arrive at the appointed time. That done, she walked out onto the balcony and stood with her arms folded across her breasts, looking down at Athens.

She knew the SOBs were down there, looking for Nile Barrabas, but she also knew that if Barrabas had been taken by an enemy, he was either dead, or far from Athens. He could be anywhere.

With a shudder, she went back into the room, just as Lee Hatton came in the outer door. Erika looked at her hopefully, but Hatton simply shook her head and gave a helpless shrug.

"Where did you look?" Erika asked.

"I questioned the hotel staff. No one saw him leave."

"That's not possible. Nile is not the kind of man to go unnoticed. Someone is lying."

"I've considered that," Hatton said, "but whoever it is, he's a good liar. No one appeared to be hiding anything."

"Perhaps someone else should question the staff," Erika said.

"You might be right."

"Please—" Erika was immediately apologetic "—I didn't mean..."

"I know you didn't," Hatton said.

The next to arrive were Claude Hayes and Liam O'Toole. Erika gave them the same hopeful look, but they gave her back the same helpless shrug as Lee.

"We checked the immediate area around the hotel," Hayes said, "talked to as many people as we could. No one saw anything."

"What now?" Erika asked.

"We'll go out again," O'Toole said, "at about the same time the colonel went out. Maybe then we'll find someone who saw him. That's all we can do for now."

Room service finally arrived with a cold spread on two food carts, and while Hatton and O'Toole were eating, the freshened-up Jessup arrived.

"Nanos? Billy Two?" he said.

"Not back yet," O'Toole said. "They were going up to the Acropolis."

Jessup nodded and eyed the food on the carts. At that moment Nanos and Billy Two returned.

"Nothing on the colonel," Nanos said, "but we did find out one thing."

"What?" Jessup asked.

"Two men were killed up at the Acropolis last night."

"How?"

"They were shot."

"Who did you find this out from?" O'Toole asked.

"Just an Athenian who likes to talk to tourists," Nanos replied.

"I'll have to check with the police and see what they have," Jessup said, "just in case there's a connection."

"Hell," Nanos said, "maybe the colonel ran into trouble and killed them. Maybe he's in some Greek jail right now."

"I doubt it, but I'll check." Jessup looked at Erika. "I have to make some calls."

"Use the phone in the bedroom," she offered. He nodded and left the room.

"I agree we should go out later and try again for something on the colonel," Billy Two said. His reasoning was the same as O'Toole's. The best time to walk the streets and ask questions was at the time Barrabas would have been on the streets.

"How many people would have been out at that time?" Erika asked.

"It only takes one," O'Toole told her.

Nanos walked to the food cart and helped himself to some cold cuts. There was a bucket filled with ice and bottles of beer; he opened a bottle.

"I'll be out on the balcony for a few minutes," Billy Two announced.

"What's he going out there for?" O'Toole asked Nanos.

"He needs privacy to ask Hawk Spirit for his help."

O'Toole thought a moment, then shrugged. "Well, why not? We can use all the help we can get."

The SOBs busied themselves with cold cuts and beer, each alone with his or her thoughts. Where was Barrabas? If, indeed, someone had taken him prisoner, who...and how?

Why was a question, too, although less important. In all their lives the same *why* was forever present—revenge. Revenge from someone they had done damage to in the past.

And God knew that Nile Barrabas had done damage to enough people in the past—enough *bad* people—that one of them might want to come back and take revenge.

"Why?" Erika suddenly said aloud.

All of the SOBs looked over at her, with the exception of Billy Two, who was on his knees on the balcony, looking up at the stars—or at the great Hawk-God.

"There could be a lot of reasons," Lee Hatton said gently. She was speaking the words that the others had been thinking. "I don't think the why of it is very important, Erika. Not important enough to occupy our time right now. What we have to worry about finding out now is *who* took him, and *where* they took him."

"But if no one saw him—"

"No one admits to seeing him," Liam O'Toole said. "Somebody could be lying."

"Why?" Erika asked again.

"Money," Alex Nanos said.

"Or fear," Claude Hayes suggested.

"What we have to do," Hatton said, "is show them more money. Or more fear."

"Speaking of money," Liam O'Toole said, "if it comes to that, where are we going to get it?"

They all looked at Walker Jessup, who had just reentered the room.

"Hey," he said, "I'm here on a personal basis. The government is not going to come up with a large sum of money to save just one man, no matter who he is."

"Don't they call you the Fixer?" Lee Hatton said. "Fix this!"

Jessup opened his mouth to answer, then thought better of it and closed it again.

"I can make some more calls," he said finally, "but I can't make any promises."

"What about the calls you just made?" O'Toole asked.

"I'm waiting for an answer. After I get it I'll make the other calls." He cast a look at the cold cuts, which were swiftly being depleted. "I'll go to my room and use my phone. I left my number."

After he left, Erika said, "I must make a call, as well."

"To whom?" Hatton asked.

"My brother. Gunther will want to help."

"With money?" Nanos asked.

"With anything," she said, and went into the other room.

They all knew that Gunther Dykstra, a big, blond giant of a man, owned a rock club in Amsterdam, but that his real business—and Erika's—was smuggling.

"Well, if Jessup and Erika take care of the money end," O'Toole said, "that leaves the rest of it up to us."

"And what's that?" Hatton asked.

"Getting a line on who took him, and where," O'Toole replied. "Shall we cover the same ground later?"

"Let's alternate," Hatton replied. "I think the hotel staff might respond to someone a little . . ."

"Uglier?" Nanos said.

"Exactly," she replied.

"That means you, Claude," Nanos said.

"Very funny," Hayes said.

"I mean it. You're big and black, and to some of these Greeks in the hotel, you'll be ugly.

Hayes glared at him.

"They don't know the beautiful inner you, as we do," O'Toole said. "I'll take Lee with me, Alex, you and Billy can cover the Acropolis again."

"Me, Billy and Hawk Spirit."

"Three's a crowd?" O'Toole asked.

"It probably would be, if I could see the ol' Hawk Spirit," Nanos said. "I'll just have to take Billy's word that he's there."

None of them laughed. The big Osage had accomplished some amazing things since his "alliance" with the Hawk Spirit.

"Anybody want to catch a nap before we go out again?" O'Toole asked.

Nobody responded to that suggestion. Despite the amount of traveling they had all done to get there, none of them was particularly sleepy.

"In that case," O'Toole said, "I'll order some more food."

BARRABAS WOKE WITH A START, aware that he was still tied in an upright position. How had he fallen asleep? What was the last thing he remembered?

Oh yes, the cries of a woman—cries of pleasure.

He wondered if the woman knew anything about his presence in the cellar beneath her. If she did, it certainly wasn't inhibiting her sex life.

Barrabas moved his head cautiously, side to side, then back and forth. The pain from the blow that had felled him had lessened considerably, and he felt alert, no longer concussed. He was thirsty and hungry, which was a good sign, and his limbs were painfully cramped.

He tested his bonds again and found them as tight as ever. Using his tongue he tried to rid himself of the gag, which had become soaked with saliva, but whoever had tied him knew his business.

He blinked his eyes behind the blindfold. They felt gritty and hot.

He took several deep, calming breaths, letting them out through his nose instead of trying to force them around the gag.

His best course now was to try to relax and get as much rest as possible. When rescue came, he was going to have to be in shape to help—or, at least, not hinder his rescuers.

Barrabas had no doubt that Erika had contacted the SOBs by now. They'd be at her hotel, checking the area, checking with the staff. He tried to think back to that night—last night? Two nights ago? How long had he been here? Had he seen anyone—or had anyone seen him—who might give the SOBs something to go on?

He was retracing his steps in his mind when he heard footsteps. It sounded as if they were on stone, perhaps coming downstairs from the floor above. They got closer, until he was sure someone was right outside the door. There was the scrape of a key in a lock, and then a door opened.

He felt a breeze on his face and took deep breaths of the fresh air.

Someone entered the room and closed the door, cutting off the current of air before it could do much to freshen the stale atmosphere of the cellar. Breathing through his nose, Barrabas became aware of a new scent in the room, pleasantly sweet, almost exotic.

He knew there was a woman in the room with him even before her hand came down gently on the back of his neck, stroking him with firm, cool fingers.

He sat still while both hands moved over his neck, around to the front to unfasten the buttons of his shirt. Whoever she was, she was running her hands over the hard muscles of his chest. She leaned over him and he felt her hair brush him. He knew it must be long hair.

"Wha—" he started, but she stopped him immediately.

"Shh," she said, rubbing her hand over him.

She continued to stroke his chest, her chin resting on the top of his head. He could feel her breath ruffling the hair on top of his head.

He wondered why she didn't speak. If she was the woman whose cry of pleasure he had heard before he slept, he knew she had a voice. Was she afraid of someone upstairs hearing them? Or did she just not want him to hear her voice?

Suddenly there was the sound of a car door closing, and her hands and chin jerked away. He knew then that she was downstairs with him because there had been no one upstairs, but now someone was returning.

She pressed her soft lips against his ear and whispered, "I will come back."

Hurriedly she ran from the room and locked the door. He heard her footsteps as she ran upstairs, and then another door closed.

Her scent lingered in the room.

Who she was did not matter, at the moment. That she would return did. It gave him something to look forward to.

There was something else about her, though, that stayed with him. Her voice. Although she'd only whispered four words to him, her voice had sounded familiar.

It took a few moments, but it suddenly came to him. Her voice had sounded almost exactly like Lee Hatton's.

3

The SOBs went out again at four a.m.

Claude Hayes talked to the hotel staff. O'Toole had advised him not to smile and to frown a lot. Nanos added that Hayes looked especially mean when he was scowling. Hayes told them to go fuck themselves, but with each person he interviewed he found himself scowling more and more.

By the time he got to the desk clerk his scowl was at its meanest. Somebody was lying, because Barrabas—tall, muscular and sporting a shock of white hair—could not possibly have walked through this hotel, at any time of the day or night, without someone noticing him.

"Were you working night before last?" Hayes asked.

The clerk was a slender young man who spoke excellent English, which was probably one of the reasons he'd gotten the job.

"Yes, sir," he replied politely.

"Until what time?"

"Until six in the morning."

"I'm going to show you a photograph," Hayes said. "I want you to tell me if you saw this man leave the hotel at any time while you were on duty." Hayes realized his polite tone was not making a mean impression, so he accompanied it with a deep scowl.

"Uh, of course, s-sir," the clerk said.

Hayes produced the photo. "Do you remember this man?"

"Yes, sir. He has been a guest of the hotel for the entire week."

"Yes, he has, but I want you to specifically recall that night, into the morning hours. Did you see him leave the hotel?"

"A lady has asked me these same questions—" the young man started to say.

"And now I'm asking," Hayes said. "Did you see him leave?"

"I—do not wish any trouble."

"There's won't be any trouble, sport," Hayes said. "Not if you answer my question. Did you see him?"

"I—yes, I saw him."

"Leaving the hotel?"

"Yes."

"At what time?"

"It was about a quarter after four."

"How can you be so sure?"

"I was listening to the radio," the man said, indicating a small portable radio farther along on the desk. Hayes noticed that it was on now, the volume turned low.

"Did he speak to you?"

"No, sir."

"Now, this is very important," Hayes said. "Did you see anyone leave right after him?"

"No."

"Did you see him return?"

"I went off duty at six."

"Did you see him return by then?"

"I did not."

"Why didn't you tell the woman this?"

The man shrugged. "He is staying with a woman," he replied, "and it was not she who was asking me about him. I thought, perhaps, this woman was another lover, or a wife. I did not wish to cause trouble."

"I see," Hayes stared at the clerk a little longer, until he began to fidget, but Hayes finally was satisfied that the man was telling the truth.

Meanwhile, O'Toole and Hatton walked the streets on all sides of the hotel, and didn't see a soul. They widened their circle then, to take in several blocks, but encountered no one.

"Doesn't anyone in Athens walk their dog?" Lee said aloud.

"Maybe nobody in Athens has a dog."

"I hope Claude is doing better with the hotel staff than I did," she said. "Someone had to have seen him leave the hotel."

"We'll find out when we get back."

Athens nightlife—which was, to say the least, hot—comprised two separate time periods. From seven p.m. to midnight most of the clubs, restaurants and casinos were filled with vacationing tourists. From midnight to two p.m. the Athenians themselves turned out to have a good time. Especially a certain type who can really enjoy himself.

Actually, certain kind of Athenian men—the tough kind who can "take their liquor"—to show how good a time they are having will start to break plates. No doubt this evolved from unintentional beginnings until it became almost a custom, and although the actual plate breaking has been outlawed, in its place the revelers now throw flowers or plastic items.

The SOB duo were walking the streets after four a.m., and since most of the night spots had closed at two a.m., the tourists and the Athenians had gone to bed.

"I wonder if there are any after-hours clubs in Athens," said Liam O'Toole, who knew where most of the after-hours joints were in New York.

"We'd better get back and see what the others have found," Hatton said glumly, and O'Toole agreed.

As they were walking back to the hotel O'Toole commented, "We're being followed."

"I know," Hatton said. "What do we do?"

"Nothing, for now. Let's just get back and compare notes."

Nanos and Billy Two were being followed, too, in a most obvious fashion.

"I can't believe he's so sloppy," Nanos said.

"It can mean only one thing," Billy Two said.

Nanos was expecting the big Osage to attribute it to the will of the Hawk Spirit, but Billy surprised him.

"He wants us to see him."

Nanos looked at the big Indian and said, "You're right, but why?"

Their visit to the Acropolis had yielded nothing. There was simply no one there at four a.m. When Barrabas had been taken—and they were acting on that assumption—he and his captors had to have been the only souls there.

On the way to the hotel they passed the parliament building, which had once been called the Royal Palace.

The other three sides of Constitution Square were flanked by office buildings and hotels. One of the main attractions of the square was the cafés lining every side and also in the center. During the day, it was estimated that over three thousand chairs were set out in the square.

At this time of night the area was deserted and there was not a chair in sight. Still, a tail who did not want to be spotted could have found some way of avoiding detection. This one had made not the slightest attempt.

"We could ask him why," Billy Two said.

"Not now," Nanos said. "First let's see what the others have to say."

Billy Two nodded, and the two ignored their follower as they continued on their way to the hotel.

As Nanos and Billy Two entered, Walker Jessup looked up from the sofa where he sat. O'Toole and Hatton were standing nearby, holding cups of coffee. Over by the balcony door, Hayes, too, was drinking coffee.

"Barrabas is not in jail," Jessup announced. "My contact checked. There's nothing to connect him to the killing of those two men at the Acropolis."

"Do they have any suspects?" O'Toole asked.

"None. The police are assuming the shooting was the result of an argument, possibly over a woman."

"That's one way to close an argument," O'Toole remarked. "Were they drunken tourists?"

Jessup shook his head. "The dead men were locals."

"Where is Erika?" Nanos asked.

"Asleep in the bedroom," Hatton said. "We promised to wake her if there were any developments. Are there?"

"Maybe," Nanos said.

"What do you mean, maybe?" Jessup asked.

Nanos looked at the others and asked, "Has anyone else been followed?"

"We were," O'Toole said.

"I didn't leave the hotel," Hayes said.

"How did you spot the tail?" Nanos asked O'Toole.

"Easy," O'Toole said. "He wasn't even trying not to be seen."

"The same with ours."

Billy Two had gone over to where the coffeepot was and reached for the pitcher of water next to it.

"Obviously," he said, pouring himself a glass of cold water, "someone *wants* us to know we're being followed."

"But why?" Jessup asked, frowning.

"And who is the 'someone'?" O'Toole added. "Could whoever took Barrabas have sent us these obvious tails?"

"I can see why they might want to keep an eye on us," Walker Jessup said, "but why make the tails so obvious?"

"They must want us to know that they know we're here," Hatton suggested.

"They know we're here, but do they know who we are?" O'Toole asked. "What do they know about the Soldiers of Barrabas? Or do they simply think we're friends of the colonel's?"

"If they know about the SOBs—" Nanos looked at Jessup "—what do they know about you?"

"Those are good questions," Jessup said. "Maybe if we asked them, they'd give us some answers."

"Let's think about that," O'Toole said.

"You think about it." Jessup rubbed his eyes. "I'm too tired to think."

"You're right," O'Toole agreed. "We can all use some sleep. Let's turn in and meet here again in a few hours. Say eight a.m.?"

Everyone was in favor of that.

Nanos and Billy Two were sharing a room, as were O'Toole and Hayes. Walker Jessup had a single room. Lee Hatton also had a room of her own, but she decided to stay with Erika.

"Who knows?" she said. "Maybe the colonel will come walking in."

"You'll let us know if he does," Walker Jessup said without conviction.

She nodded. "Right after I wring his neck."

BARRABAS WOKE UP. If by nothing other than instinct, he knew it was morning. His back was aching from sitting up in the chair for so long—for how long? He was surprised that he had been able to fall asleep.

He could detect no light from behind his blindfold, but there was that fresh sea smell in the air.

If he reckoned by his waking hours, he had been in captivity two days. But if he had been unconscious for greater lengths of time than he figured, then it was longer than that.

Surely by this time the other SOBs were in Athens, trying to track him.

He hoped that someone had left some tracks somewhere.

JOSHUA, TOO, AWOKE, aware of the woman's hip pressed against his.

This was a key day for Joshua. His men would be arriving today, sometime in the afternoon. They were not the men gathered by Wolenski, but rather men whom Joshua himself had chosen. They had been contacted and told that they would be sent for when the time was right.

Now that Joshua had Barrabas as his prisoner, the time was right.

The woman moaned and rolled over, moving her hip away from him. He took that opportunity to rise. He was naked, and left the small house without dressing. There were few facilities in the house, and a dip into the ocean each morning served as his daily shower.

At the moment, Joshua and the woman—and Barrabas—were the only inhabitants of the island, but that would change within the next few hours.

The six men who were on their way to the island were the best fighting men he knew, mercenaries all. He was paying them a lot of money to become his own private army.

As he submerged himself in the Ionian sea he knew that if his plan worked—and he had no doubt that it would—it would be worth every penny.

JULIANNE GOT OUT OF BED after Joshua had left the house, then went to the window and watched as the scarred man entered the water. She thought about the man in the basement.

She thought of the man she had slept with as Joshua, even though it was not his real name. She didn't know his real name, and he would answer no questions about it.

Joshua certainly satisfied her in almost every way possible. He was a marvelous lover, and he kept her fed and clothed, though his preference for bikinis meant she usually wore a bathing suit.

But she was afraid of him.

She knew, too, that Joshua feared the man in the cellar.

That made this man, Barrabas, almost irresistible to Julianne. If Joshua caught her with him—even talking to him—he would kill her, and yet that danger made it even more exciting to sneak down there and...

Joshua had a radio setup on the island, away from the house, and it was when he went there that she would have her next chance to go downstairs. When Joshua's men arrived she'd have even more time; he had already said that he'd be busy with them, training them, getting them ready for what he called "the ultimate battle."

Julianne was also naked and she ran her hands over her body, then stretched them over her head, pulling her entire body taut.

Last night, for the first time, while Joshua made love to her, she had thought about another man.

Barrabas.

WHEN ERIKA AWOKE that morning it was with a gasp. Her sharp intake of breath was so loud that Lee Hatton heard it in the next room.

"Erika?" Hatton poked her head into the bedroom.

Erika sat up in bed, stared at Lee and frowned. Lee knew Erika was not focusing properly at that moment.

"Erika, it's Lee Hatton."

Slowly recognition dawned and Erika Dykstra re-laxed.

"Are you awake?" Hatton asked.

"I'm awake."

"Would you like breakfast?"

"Yes."

"It'll be ready after your shower."

"Yes, all right," Erika said dully. "Thank you."

As Hatton left the room, it occurred to Erika, just for a moment, that she had been better off in the some-what muddled state of her first waking, when she had had no memory of the incidents of the past two days.

Now the memories had all come back to her. Slowly she got out of bed, her proud, firm body slumped de-jectedly.

If only she didn't love Barrabas so fiercely, she thought as she turned on the water for a shower.

Hatton called room service as soon as she left Erika, and ordered breakfast for two, as soon as possible. Then she stepped out onto the balcony, and looked out over Athens, bright and beautiful in the morning sun.

Where was Nile Barrabas? she wondered. Some-where in this lovely historic city, or on one of the thou-sands of Greek islands? Or in another country altogether, by now?

Or dead?

WHEN WALKER JESSUP WOKE he was ravenous. He, too, called room service for breakfast, then took a long shower. In the shower he started thinking about weap-ons.

If Barrabas had been taken, and was alive, the SOBs would need weapons to get him back. They had not brought any with them, so they were going to have to buy them. For that they needed money.

Last night on the phone Jessup, in his role as the Fixer, had managed to call in a few favors. Today, at the nearest American Express office, he would be picking up some money, but not nearly as much as the SOBs would need. The rest would have to come from Erika Dykstra's brother, Gunther. When she had called last night he had not been available. She had left him an urgent message to call back, and they hoped he would do so today.

Still, with the money he collected from the Amex office, he could send O'Toole and Nanos out—O'Toole because he was, technically, Barrabas's second in command, and Nanos because he was Greek—and see what they could come up with in the way of weapons.

The overriding concern for Jessup, however, was what they would do once they were outfitted. If they failed to get a line on Barrabas, weapons would be useless, even in the hands of the greatest mercenary fighting unit in the world.

Drying his huge body with a thin hotel towel, Walker Jessup looked at his reflection in the fogged-up mirror and said aloud, "Where the hell are you, Nile?"

HUNGER GNAWED at Barrabas's stomach like something alive. He was now convinced that he had no serious injuries; his concern now was nourishment, and getting the circulation going in his hands and feet. When he was rescued he did not want to have to be carried by anyone. He wanted to be handed a gun and be able to hold his own.

He tested his bonds. As tight as ever. When the woman came back, would she talk to him? Would she take out the gag and let him talk to her? Could he persuade her to let him go, or at least to loosen the ropes so that his blood could circulate properly?

What was her part in this abduction? He had been assuming she was the wife or lover of the man who had captured him. Was he not giving her enough credit? Perhaps it was she who had engineered his capture. If so, for what purpose?

Certainly not to kill him. If that was the aim of his captors, he'd be dead already. They were keeping him alive for some reason... but what?

There had been very few times in his life that Nile Barrabas had felt physically and mentally helpless, but this was certainly one of them.

He was glad that the hunger in his stomach was so insistent.

If there was fear nestling in his belly, he couldn't feel it.

4

The SOBs and Jessup were having coffee with Erika in her suite when the phone rang. She went into the other room to answer it.

"Let's hope that's her brother," Jessup said.

They were all present except for Billy Two. Nanos had not heard him go out, but the big Osage had not been in the room when Nanos woke.

"Let's get back to business," O'Toole said. "Who knows any arms dealers here in Greece? Alex?"

"Sorry, Liam. I was born in Greece, but not in Athens, and I haven't been here very much of late. Not the way we travel."

"Anyone else?" O'Toole asked.

No one answered. During the silence there was a knock at the door. Hayes, the nearest to it, opened it and admitted Billy Two.

"Where the hell have you been?" Nanos demanded.

"I went out to do some scouting," Billy Two said.

"What did you see?" O'Toole asked.

"Our tails are still out there."

"How many?"

Billy Two replied, "One for each of us."

"Are they making any attempt to stay hidden?" Claude Hayes asked.

"None. I didn't even have to look hard."

"Shit," Jessup said. "What the hell is going on?"

"A while ago someone suggested asking them," Lee Hatton recalled. "Why don't we?"

"I've got a better idea," O'Toole said.

"What?" Jessup asked.

"Why don't *we* follow *them*?"

"How do we do that?"

"Well, not all of us," O'Toole continued, "just Billy."

"Explain," Billy Two said.

"Is the same man who followed you and Alex last night out there?"

"No."

"Then that means they're taking shifts," O'Toole said. "All we have to do is wait for one of them to go off shift, and then Billy follows him home."

"And that's when we start asking questions," Hatton said.

O'Toole nodded. "That's when."

At that point Erika walked into the room. "That was my brother, Gunther. He's wiring some money to me at the American Express office."

"We'll have to thank him," Lee said.

"There's no need for that," Erika explained. "The money he's wiring is mine."

Nobody had a response to that.

"He gave me something else," Erika went on.

"What?" Jessup asked.

"A name." She held out a piece of paper. O'Toole, the closest to her, took it from her.

"Demetrius Kontiza," O'Toole read aloud.

"He's an arms dealer," Erika said.

"Anybody know him?" O'Toole asked.

He was greeted by blank stares and shaking heads.

"Well, we've got a phone number here," O'Toole said, "and beggars can't be choosers. All right, uh, Mr. Jessup, you'll be picking up the money?"

"Erika will have to come with me to sign for hers," Jessup said.

"Right," O'Toole said.

"How do we ditch the tails?" Jessup asked.

"We don't," O'Toole said. "We'll let them go where we go. At least that way, we know where they are."

"Is that safe?" Erika asked.

O'Toole looked at Erika. "If they wanted to do any of us harm, they would have moved by now. They're just keeping us under surveillance for someone else."

"Who?" she asked.

"After we're set with the money and the weapons we need," O'Toole said, "we'll be in a position to ask that question of someone who can give us the right answer."

"Do you plan to feed him?"

Joshua looked at Julianne. "Are you worried about him?"

"No," she said, "I'm concerned about you. He's the key to your revenge. Do you want him to die down there?"

He frowned. "You're right," he said. "But I've got to go to the radio. Will you feed him for me?"

"If you wish."

He moved to her and put his hand beneath her chin. "I know it will not be pleasant for you. When my men arrive I'll have one of them look after feeding him."

"I will do it for you," she said.

She was aware of how powerful the hand holding her chin was. He could crush the life out of her just as easily as he now held her chin.

Still, if danger had not appealed to her, she would not have been there with him now.

In the cellar, Barrabas heard footsteps on the stairs. For want of something else to do, he counted the steps. When he reached thirteen he heard the key in the lock. He noticed for the first time that the door, when it opened, sounded very heavy.

Once again he could feel fresh air waft across his face, and with it the scent of the woman's perfume. He smelled something else, as well.

Food.

He heard the door close. Her footsteps crossed the room to him. She took eight steps to reach him. If he was seated in the center of the room, then it was sixteen paces wide. If she was a tall woman, and her strides were—

His calculations were cut off when she touched his face.

"I am going to take off the gag," she said. She was not whispering. He was struck again by how similar her voice was to Lee Hatton's, except for the slight accent.

"I am doing so to feed you," she went on. "If you try to speak I will put the gag back and you will not eat. If you understand, please nod."

He nodded.

"Very well." She slid the gag from his mouth.

He was tempted to try to speak, but the smell of the food had sharpened his hunger pangs, and he merely licked his lips to moisten them.

"Open," she said.

He opened his mouth and she put something into it. It was cool and sweet, and tasted like a kind of melon. Although he would have preferred steak and eggs, he didn't complain. He chewed it eagerly, swallowed and then opened his mouth again.

He felt the next piece ease between his lips, but before he could close his mouth she pulled the food away, teasing him.

"Open," she said then. He did so, but it was not a piece of fruit that slid into his mouth.

It was her tongue.

WALKER JESSUP AND ERIKA DYKSTRA left the hotel together, and their respective tails immediately fell in behind them.

Claude Hayes then came out of the hotel and fell in behind Jessup, Dykstra and the tails. The man assigned to follow him moved into place and dogged the footsteps of the black man.

A few moments later Lee Hatton and Liam O'Toole headed off in the same direction as the others. When their assigned tails followed them, they formed a procession that would have seemed comical to an observer who knew what was going on. Hatton remarked on the fact to Liam O'Toole.

"This will let them know that we know they're there, and that we can play games just as well as they can," he said.

"What if they don't like the games we're playing?"

"Then they'll make a move. But I don't think that will happen. I'm betting they have to wait for orders before they can move."

The procession arrived at the Amex office, where Jessup and Erika withdrew their money. While they were inside, the SOBs and their tails had to wait outside, trying not to bump into one another.

"This gets more and more farcical," Hatton said to O'Toole. "If I weren't so worried about the colonel I'd be laughing my head off."

"I know. These guys are pathetic. If a move is going to be made against us, it isn't going to be by these fellas."

"Why didn't you go and see this Demetrius while Jessup and Erika were picking up the money? Certainly he wouldn't expect cash to change hands at the first meeting."

"No," O'Toole said, "but I'd need at least a flash roll to be taken seriously."

"Will you be going alone?"

"No, I'll take Alex with me, just in case there's a language problem."

"Surely you'll want to shake the guys following the two of you before you go."

"Oh, yeah," O'Toole said. "We'll shake them, all right. I don't anticipate any problem with that."

"What do you anticipate problems with?"

O'Toole looked at Hatton and found she was studying his face intently. "You really want to know?"

"Of course."

He took a deep breath. "I don't know how we'll find him, Lee. If one of these tails talks, fine, but if it was me running them, I wouldn't tell them any more than they needed to know."

"So you don't think they know where he is?"

"If it was me," he said again, "I wouldn't even have told them about him."

"So if they can't help us, what do we do next?"

He shrugged.

At that moment Jessup and Erika came out of the Amex office.

"Let's go," O'Toole said.

They followed Jessup and Erika and the procession wound its way back to the hotel.

BARRABAS DIDN'T UNDERSTAND IT, but he realized that the kisses were the price he had to pay for the food. Toward the end she simply put the fruit in her own mouth and fed it to him that way. In spite of his situation, he found that her scent, her mouth, the nearness of her body aroused him, which was just one more thing he had to endure.

"There," she said, "it's all gone. I have to put the gag back in now."

"But—" he started, but she put her hand over his mouth.

"I don't want to, but I must." Before he could say anything else she removed her hand and replaced the gag.

"I wish I could help you with this—" she brushed her hand across his crotch, "but there's no time. Maybe next time." She touched his face and whispered again, "Maybe next time."

If there is a next time, Barrabas thought as she walked across the room, through the door and up the stairs again.

Yesterday she had said "I'll be back," and she had kept her promise. Now she said, "Maybe."

Had he just blown his only chance?

He didn't think so. For some reason, this woman seemed drawn to him. That much was obvious from the way she'd acted, as if she wanted to devour him the way he was devouring the fruit.

Barrabas knew he was attractive to women—he'd had his fair share of beauties, none more beautiful than Erika—but the mysterious woman who sounded like Lee Hatton seemed to feel more than just an attraction. Whatever it was, he thought it would bring her back to him again.

He thought about Erika then, which did nothing to alleviate the discomfort in his crotch. How was she doing? Had he once again drawn her into something dangerous? And if he had, what kind of damage would be done to her this time?

By now, at least, she'd be with friends. Hatton would probably be able to help her emotionally while all the SOBs tried to figure out their next move.

Barrabas knew he hadn't run into anyone on the streets of Athens that night, so he wondered how they would possibly manage to get a line on him.

But he also knew that O'Toole and the others had accomplished some pretty amazing things in the past, both with him and without him. Maybe Billy Two's Hawk Spirit would lead them to him.

You listening, Hawk Spirit?

BACK IN ERIKA'S HOTEL SUITE the SOBs split up the work.

"Alex, you'll come with me to see the arms guy," O'Toole said.

None of the others objected to O'Toole's take-charge tone. Somebody had to take up the reins in Barrabas's absence, and they accepted O'Toole's temporary leadership.

"Right," Nanos agreed.

"Billy, our tails are going to be pretty upset over losing us. At least one of them is going to have to go get more instructions."

"And *I* tail *him*," Billy finished.

"That's right."

"And the rest of us?" Jessup asked.

"Claude will back up Billy, in case things get nasty."

"That leaves me, Hatton and Erika," Jessup said.

"You'll just have to sit tight."

"I want to do something," Erika said.

"So do I," Hatton added.

But Jessup didn't argue. Fieldwork was not his specialty, though on occasion he participated, when he had to. He was simply not built for it. Now he addressed O'Toole. "I've got something for you."

"What?"

Jessup reached into his pocket and brought out a .32 caliber Heckler & Koch automatic.

"Where'd you get that?"

"Brought it along," he big man said. "You forget, Nanos, Billy Two and I didn't come in on a commercial flight." Jessup held out the gun to O'Toole. "You might need it."

"Keep it," O'Toole said. "*You* might need it."

"Up here?"

"When Alex, Billy Two, Claude and I disappear, somebody might get the bright idea to come up here. In fact, I suggest you three not even stay in this room."

"We could go to mine," Hatton volunteered.

"Are you registered under your own name?" O'Toole asked her.

"Yes. I didn't see any reason—"

O'Toole waved her explanation away. He looked at Walker Jessup. "Am I correct in assuming that you did not register under your own name?"

"You are," Jessup said. "Old habits die hard."

"Then you three wait for us in your room," O'Toole said.

"Good idea." Jessup heaved his bulk up from the chair.

"Now?" Erika said.

"Now," O'Toole replied.

"Let me get some things to take with me."

"You won't be there long," O'Toole said. "Lee?"

"Come on, Erika," Hatton said. "We all have to work together to find the colonel."

Reluctantly Erika allowed herself to be escorted from the room.

Nanos could never resist a joke. "Anybody wants to find them, all they've got to do is follow room service."

"That's funny, Alex," O'Toole said, "but not really fair. Jessup is a good man, and smart. He won't do anything to jeopardize their safety."

"I know."

"When do we start?" Billy Two asked.

"Now," O'Toole said. "Alex and I will find another way out of the hotel."

"Think they'll have the back covered?" Hayes asked.

"They don't," Billy Two said. "At least they didn't have this morning when I checked."

"Simpletons," O'Toole said, "but whoever is behind them is not a simpleton."

"How do we know that?" Hayes asked.

"They got the colonel, didn't they?" Nanos asked.

No one had an answer to that.

Once O'Toole and Nanos had left the hotel, leaving their tails behind, they forgot about them.

Gunther Dykstra had provided Demetrius Kontiza's telephone number. O'Toole decided to call from a pay phone. Nanos stood outside the booth.

The phone was answered on the second ring. *"Herete,"* a man answered.

"Hello," O'Toole echoed. "I am calling Demetrius Kontiza."

There was a pause, and then the man said in English, "There is no one here by that name."

The fact that the man spoke English told O'Toole that he did indeed have the right number.

"Please," he said respectfully. "I was told by a friend that Mr. Kontiza was a great man who could help me with my troubles."

"What kind of troubles?"

"I am having a problem," O'Toole said, "with my arms."

"Mr. Kontiza is not a doctor."

"I know that."

There was another pause.

"You said a friend recommended Mr. Kontiza?"

"Yes."

"What friend?"

"I cannot say his name."

"You may speak freely," the man said. O'Toole took this to mean that the phone at the other end was clean.

He had to assume that was also true of the phone booth, chosen at random.

Still, he did not want to speak Erika's brother's full name. "My friend's name is Gunther."

"Gunther? That is all?"

"Yes."

"And what does this Gunther do?"

O'Toole thought a moment, then said, "He deals in rock and roll."

"Rock and roll?" the man asked, as if unsure that he had heard right.

"Yes," O'Toole repeated, "rock and roll."

A pause, then, "Please wait."

O'Toole had to feed more coins into the phone while waiting, but the man finally came back on. He spoke an address, and hung up.

"Wait—" O'Toole said, but it was too late. He hung up and stepped out of the booth.

"What happened?"

"I got an address," O'Toole said. "Number One Tositsa Street."

"What's there?"

"Damned if I know. That's all I got."

"Well, where is it?"

"Don't you know?" O'Toole asked. "This is your town."

"This is not my town," Nanos said. "I was born in a fishing village, damn it. My father has never even been to Athens."

"So what do we do?"

"We ask an Athenian," Nanos said.

"You pick one," O'Toole said, nodding at the people going by them in either direction.

Nanos stopped a woman in her forties who was obviously not a tourist and asked in Greek if she knew what was at One Tositsa Street. The woman looked at him as if he was crazy, responded shortly and then went on her way.

"Silly me," Nanos said.

"What did she say?"

"One Tositsa Street is the address of the National Archaeological Museum."

"And you didn't know that? What kind of a Greek are you?"

"I knew it sounded familiar," Nanos mumbled.

Although the museum's address was Tositsa Street, the main entrance actually faced Patission Avenue.

From Patission Avenue they approached the museum through a spacious garden surrounded by cafés beneath palm trees. The area was crowded with tourists, and sight-seeing buses were disgorging more visitors into the area.

"How are we supposed to recognize this Kontiza, if he shows up?" Nanos asked.

"Damned if I know."

"I knew I should have made that call."

"Let's just go inside."

They climbed a sweeping marble staircase to the classical facade of the entrance. From a huge entry hall they continued into the Mycenaean hall. They couldn't help but be impressed by the treasures on display there: intricate gold and silver dagger blades, swords, breastplates, gold-leaf portrait masks, libation cups and a variety of representations of mammals and birds. Everything in the room dated from 1250 B.C.

"This is amazing!" Nanos said.

"You're Greek and you've never been here?"

"You spend a lot of time in New York," Nanos said. "Have you ever visited the Statue of Liberty?"

They fell silent and continued on.

In other exhibit areas they saw a bronze statue of Poseidon, poised to hurl his trident, and a bronze head of Hermes; dating from 450 B.C.

They went on to view fine pottery, gold rings and bracelets, and eventually made their way back to the entry hall.

"Well, this has all been very enlightening," O'Toole said, "but we haven't accomplished what we came here for."

"What do we do now?" Nanos asked. "Walk through again?"

"As impressive as this all has been, I don't think so."

"Out front, then?"

"Why not?"

They had almost reached the exit when a man intercepted them. He was not large but was well built, and he was simply, almost shabbily dressed.

"You are Gunther's friends?" he asked in accented English.

"We are," O'Toole said.

"Did you enjoy the museum?"

O'Toole nodded. "Very much."

"Then perhaps you would join me outside for lunch?"

"We'd be delighted."

The man smiled and led them to a café in the center of all the hustle and bustle. They found a table. When a waiter came the man ordered ouzo for all three of them.

Nanos believed in being direct. "I hope you're finished sizing us up," he said in Greek.

"Ah! You are Greek." The man looked pleased.

Guessing what the man had just said, O'Toole interjected, "But I am not. Can we talk English?"

"Certainly, certainly," the man said.

"You are Demetrius Kontiza?"

"Jimmy. Please, my friends call me Jimmy."

"What do your business associates call you?" Nanos asked.

The man laughed. "My business associates *are* my friends. We will become friends . . . if we do business."

"And why wouldn't we do business?" O'Toole asked.

"That would depend on what you want."

"Arms."

"Arms," Jimmy Kontiza replied, "come in many sizes."

"Small arms, for now," O'Toole said. "Something larger later, perhaps."

"And, of course, you are able to pay."

"Of course." O'Toole had his flash roll, compliments of Erika Dykstra, but this was not the place to show it.

"May I ask why you need these arms?"

"You may," O'Toole said, and stopped there. This seemed to amuse Jimmy Kontiza, who smiled and said nothing further. O'Toole used the pause to study the man more closely.

He had shaggy hair, but his nails were clean and manicured. O'Toole figured the haircut and nondescript clothes were to show people he was one of the common folk. Look at me, they said, I'm just a poor

Greek trying to make a living. The nails, however, told O'Toole a different story. Poor Greeks don't have manicures, my friend, O'Toole thought.

Demetrius "Jimmy" Kontiza looked about thirty-five years old. He had flat, dark eyes that took in everything around him. Sometimes when he smiled the smile did not extend to his eyes, although his eyes had twinkled in amusement when he spoke of his business associates as friends. He had a livid, red scar on the back of his right hand, probably from a severe knife wound. As O'Toole watched him use the hand he decided that Jimmy had lost at least partial movement of two or three fingers.

"Shall we tell you what we need?" Nanos asked, breaking the silence.

"No," Kontiza said. "I am not prepared for that. I must first see what I have."

"You don't know your stock?" Nanos asked.

The man smiled, but this time his eyes did not.

"My stock varies. We will have to meet again."

"After you check us out with Gunther," O'Toole said.

"Yes."

"Well, we'd like to make a deal as soon as possible. We need the arms quickly, or we won't need them at all."

"You will hear from me this evening."

The waiter brought the ouzo and Kontiza picked up his glass. "Drink," he said.

"Can we do business?" O'Toole asked.

"Barring unforeseen difficulties," Kontiza said, referring to a lack of funds or Gunther's claiming no knowledge of the Greek and the Irishman, "we can do business."

O'Toole and Nanos picked up their ouzo and drank.

5

Once Liam O'Toole and Alex Nanos left the hotel the men following them became the problem of Billy Two and Claude Hayes.

The problem, of course, was for Billy Two and Hayes to follow their colleagues' tails without being followed by their own. They had also to keep in mind that these men were probably armed while they were not.

"Actually," Billy Two said before they left Erika's suite, "I do have a weapon."

"What?"

"Let's stop by my room before we go out."

They took the elevator down several floors to the room Billy Two was sharing with Nanos.

"Jessup wouldn't give Alex and me time to pack anything, but I was wearing this when he found us." He reached under the bed's mattress and came up with the biggest knife Hayes had ever seen.

"A Bowie knife?"

"It was my great-grandfather's."

"How did you get that past—"

"Jessup, Alex and I didn't come in on a commercial flight, remember?"

"So Jessup brought his gun, and you brought your knife."

"I'll feel better if I have this along."

He took out the knife's sheath and strapped it to his waist, then slid the blade home. He pulled his shirt out of his pants and draped it over the weapon. There was a bulge, but it was better than nothing.

"That reminds me," Hayes said.

"What?"

"We have to buy some clothes."

"I wonder how long Jessup's and Erika's money will last?" Billy Two said.

"Long enough, let's hope. Shall we get this thing on the road?"

"The back way," Billy Two said, and Hayes nodded.

No one was watching the back of the hotel. The two SOBs were able to position themselves so they could see the various tails, but not be seen by them.

Soon Hayes said, "This isn't going to work."

"What do you mean?" Billy Two asked.

"How long will it be before one of these clowns tumbles to the fact that maybe we're not all in the hotel? I think these dimwits will sit out here until hell freezes over before such a bright idea occurs to them."

"What do you suggest?" Billy Two asked.

"I'll walk by the front of the hotel," Hayes proposed, "and my tail will follow me."

"And I'll follow him."

"Right—without being seen by your tail."

"That won't be a problem," said Billy Two. "Hawk Spirit will cloak me from his view."

Hayes hadn't had to deal with as much Hawk Spirit talk as Nanos had, so he was unsure how to react to it. He simply said, "Uh, yeah."

"When we've taken him far enough from the others," Billy Two said, "we'll question him."

"Right."

"Give me some time to get into position," Billy Two cautioned. "Walk past the entrance and around the corner. There's no point in walking too far. Let's take him behind the hotel."

Billy Two and Hayes had left the hotel by a service exit, and had rigged the door so that they could get back in that same way.

"All right," Hayes said. "We'll take him up to one of our rooms."

Billy Two nodded, touched the knife at his side and was gone.

While Billy and Hayes carried out their plan, Liam O'Toole and Alex Nanos made their way back to the hotel.

"Do we try to go in the back way?" Nanos asked.

"No," O'Toole said, "let's go right in the front."

"That'll ruffle their feathers."

"Maybe it'll send one of them for instructions," O'Toole said. "Then Billy can follow him."

BARRABAS WONDERED if he'd get any lunch.

He guessed it was hours since the woman had fed him fruit for breakfast. If lunch was ever served, he hoped it would be something more solid.

To keep himself occupied Barrabas had been thinking, trying to figure out what enemy from his past could be responsible for kidnapping him. That was futile, however, because the list of people who might want revenge on him was so long.

Of course, most of those people would just kill him if they got the chance. Why would someone abduct him, tie him up like this in a cellar and just leave him there?

It had to be someone he knew, of course, to explain why his enemy hadn't even spoken to him. Whoever it was, he was biding his time.

The woman was yet another mystery. Who was she? Why had she sneaked down to see him the first time? Her second visit, to give him breakfast, must have been made with his captor's knowledge, but why that first time? Curiosity? Lust?

He'd abandoned the idea that the woman herself was in charge. He'd never known anyone with a voice like Lee Hatton's, and he didn't think this woman had just seen him on the streets of Athens and decided to kidnap him for her own pleasure.

Whoever was behind this, though, the woman seemed to be the weak link. He was going to have to work on her.

If she came back.

And *if* she let him speak.

CLAUDE HAYES WALKED past the entrance to the hotel as bold as brass and knew that he'd shocked his tail. The man hurriedly crossed the street, puzzlement plain on his face. He had to be wondering how Hayes had got out of the hotel, and why he was walking past it now.

Hayes led the inept watcher completely around the block, and when they reached the rear of the hotel, Billy Two stepped from hiding and fell in behind the man. As if he sensed the big Osage's presence, the man turned, looked behind him, then abruptly stopped. Hayes saw this and stopped, as well, turning around to face his tail.

The man knew he was in trouble now, with Hayes on one side of him and Billy Two on the other. Shouting would do no good because his colleagues were too far away to hear him.

Hayes could see that the man was trying to decide whether to run as he and Billy Two closed in on him.

"Parakalo," the man said to them. "Please!"

"Please what?" Hayes asked, close enough now to touch the man.

"Do not kill me," the man said, his voice wavering.

"I won't kill you," Hayes said, "but I can't say the same for my friend, there. He doesn't like being followed."

"I was not following him," the man pointed out. "I was following you."

"That doesn't make any difference. He's an Indian, and you all look alike to him."

"Please. *Leepoome*," the clown said, "I am sorry."

"Well, if you're sorry then maybe you'd be willing to help us."

"Help you? How?"

"Come with us," Hayes said as Billy closed his massive right hand over the man's elbow, the knife held ready in his left. "We want to ask you a few questions."

Hayes searched the man and was surprised—and disappointed—to find him unarmed.

"Where are we going?"

"Into the hotel," Hayes said. "You'll like it. It has all the modern conveniences, and you probably have to go to the bathroom."

AT THAT SAME MOMENT, O'Toole and Nanos walked down the street in front of the hotel, toward the entrance. When they reached it Nanos couldn't resist the urge to turn and wave at the watchers across the street.

"That's it," O'Toole said, "rub their noses in it."

"To hell with 'em if they can't take a joke."

When O'Toole and Nanos entered Erika's room they saw the red message light flashing on the phone.

"Now what?" Nanos asked.

"Maybe it's our friend Jimmy," O'Toole said.

"Too soon."

"Yeah, I know."

O'Toole picked up the phone, rang the front desk and gave the room number. "Do you have a message for me?"

Nanos watched O'Toole as the other man listened. O'Toole shook his head, indicating the message was not from the arms dealer.

"Thank you," he said, and hung up. "It's from Billy Two. He says we should come down to the room you're sharing with him right away."

"We should tell Jessup we're back," Nanos said.

"We can call him from your room. Come on."

BILLY TWO HAD THE POINT of his knife pressed underneath the unlucky tail's chin, keeping his head tilted upward. The man's eyes were popping out in his effort to look down at the knife.

"Now, here's the way this works," Hayes said. "I ask you a question, and if I don't like your answer, he cuts you a little."

"Parakalo..." the man whimpered.

"Then I ask you another question, and if I don't like the answer he cuts you a little more. Eventually he'll end up cutting your throat. Do you understand?"

"Yes, I understand."

"Good. Who do you work for?"

"Parakalo," the man said, "I will be killed."

"You'll be killed now if you don't answer," Hayes said. He nodded to Billy Two, who nicked the man's chin. The tiny cut hardly bled, but the man jumped.

"Let's try an easy one," Hayes said. "What's your name?"

"George."

"All right, George, who do you and your friends across the street work for?"

"They are not my friends," he said.

"Your colleagues, then. You're all following me and *my* friends, and we want to know who sent you."

At that moment there was a knock at the door. Hayes went and admitted O'Toole and Nanos.

"Who do we have here?" O'Toole asked.

"This is George," Hayes said.

"George?" O'Toole echoed. "Every diner in New York is run by a Greek named George. What's he doing here?"

"We invited him up," Hayes proceeded to explain to O'Toole how George happened to be their guest.

"The others are confused now, too, because they saw us come back," O'Toole said.

"Do you think they'll come in here?" Hayes asked.

"They'll need instructions first." O'Toole turned to Billy Two. "You'd better get down there, Billy. If one of them leaves, follow him."

"Right." Billy Two pressed the knife ever so slightly against George's neck, causing him to whimper, then put it away and left the room.

"He is crazy!" George said when Billy Two was gone.

"If you think he's crazy," O'Toole said, "wait until you see what our other friend is like."

O'Toole walked to the phone and dialed Jessup's room number. "We're in Alex's room," he said when the Fixer answered the ring. "You want to join us?"

"I'll be right with you."

O'Toole hung up the phone and turned to Hayes. "Find something to tie George's hands with."

Hayes pulled the drawstrings from the window curtains. He used them to bind George's hands behind him, and then tied his ankles together.

"What has he told you besides his name?"

"That's all," Hayes said. "We were just getting started."

There was a knock on the door then. It was Jessup.

"You're the bad guy," O'Toole told him in a low voice. Jessup's eyes flickered and he understood.

"Come on in," O'Toole said, stepping back.

Jessup entered the room, his bulk making it look considerably more crowded. "Is this one of those sons of bitches?" he roared. He crossed the room and grabbed the front of George's shirt with a meaty paw.

"Easy, take it easy!" O'Toole grabbed Jessup's wrist. He winked at the others, then cried, "I can't pull him off! Help me!"

Nanos and Hayes played along, making halfhearted efforts to pull Jessup away from the incompetent stalker.

"Jesus, he wants to kill him!" O'Toole cried.

"Help me! Help me!" George shouted, terrified.

"Pull him off!" O'Toole yelled.

Jessup shifted his grip from George's shirt to his throat, and the man's eyes bugged out with terror.

Finally O'Toole gave the others a signal and Jessup allowed them to pull him away.

"Hold on to him!" O'Toole told them.

Hayes and Nanos made a show of grabbing Jessup's arms and restraining him. Jessup did a good job of looking as if all he wanted to do was rip George's throat out.

"You'd better tell us who you work for," O'Toole advised the pathetic man. "I don't know how long they can hold him."

"Wolenski," George shouted, "we work for Stanley Wolenski!"

O'Toole looked at Hayes and Nanos, who released Jessup's arms. They all looked at Jessup.

"Who the fuck," Jessup said, "is Stanley Wolenski?"

BILLY TWO WATCHED and waited. Finally one of the men across the street broke away from the others and started to move down the street. Before Billy set out to follow him, the man had entered the phone booth on the corner. Billy waited. When the man left the booth he looked different. He had a different way of walking. He returned to the others and spoke to them, and they all looked at the hotel.

According to Billy Two's reading of their body language, these men wouldn't be going anywhere—unless it was *into* the hotel. The Osage went back to join the rest of the SOBs.

WOLENSKI STARED AT THE PHONE. The pattern had been broken, and he didn't like it. Joshua had told him to have his men follow the others whenever they left the hotel, but now it seemed they were leaving the hotel whenever they wanted—shaking off the tails and flaunting the fact.

Wolenski had told his man to tell the others to be ready. He would check with Joshua and see what he wanted them to do.

Stan Wolenski wished Joshua had given some information as to what they were getting involved in. If he knew a few details, he might have been able to make a decision on his own. Instead, he was afraid to make the slightest move for fear of angering Joshua.

Wolenski turned away from the phone and wheeled his desk chair over to the radio setup in the corner of his office. He picked up the mike and began to call out Joshua's call letters.

"BACK SO SOON?" O'Toole asked as Billy Two entered the room.

"One of them went to a phone booth, made a call and then returned to the others."

"That was it?"

"He was walking different when he came out of the booth."

"Walking different?" Nanos asked.

"Straighter, taller."

O'Toole interpreted the body language in the same way Billy Two had. "They might be getting ready to make a move."

"This one was unarmed," Claude Hayes nodded in George's direction. "I'd say we can assume the others are, as well."

Jessup looked down at George, who was still tied to the chair, and said, "Is that right?"

"Yes, yes, that is right. We were instructed not to carry weapons."

"Well, their instructions could change," O'Toole said. "Does anybody's room face the front?"

"Mine," Jessup said. "You can see across the street from my window."

"All right," O'Toole said, "let's move there."

"What about this Stanley Wolenski?" Jessup asked.

"Who is Stanley Wolenski?" Billy Two asked.

"That's what I mean," Jessup said.

"We may be able to find that out from our friend later on," O'Toole offered.

"Our friend?"

O'Toole looked at Jessup and touched his arm. "The arm doctor," he said.

"Oh."

"But who's Stanley Wolenski?" Billy Two asked again.

O'Toole turned to Nanos. "Explain it to Billy, will you?"

"Do not make a move," Joshua said.

"What?" Wolenski's voice came back to Joshua over the radio, sounding slightly tinny. "But they've spotted my men."

"If you remember," Joshua said, "they were supposed to spot your men."

"But—but they're playing games with us now."

"Do not do anything."

"One of my men is missing!"

Good, Joshua thought, very good. If they had one of Wolenski's men it wouldn't be long before they had Wolenski, too.

"I repeat, Stanley," Joshua said, "do nothing. Do you understand?"

There was a pause, then Wolenski said, "I understand."

Joshua broke the contact without further word, switched off his radio and smiled. He touched his face, but when his hand came in contact with the shiny scar tissue he jerked it away quickly. As he got to his feet, he thought about Julianne. He locked up the small radio shack and started walking back to the house.

Julianne saw him approaching from the window. She shivered slightly, as if she was cold, and when he moved past, out of her sight, she arranged herself on the windowsill the way she knew he liked. She was wearing the black bikini he had bought for her. She preferred to wear red or yellow, but he said that black went with her dark hair and eyes and her olive skin.

What it actually went with, she thought, was his soul.

WHEN THEY ALL ENTERED Jessup's room it was pretty crowded.

"Who's he?" Hatton asked. She had volunteered to stay with Erika when Jessup went to Billy Two and Nanos's room.

"Which of us were you supposed to follow?" O'Toole asked George.

George didn't answer right away so Hayes nudged him with an elbow.

"Her." The man gestured toward Hatton. "I was supposed to follow the woman."

"Meet your tail," O'Toole said to Hatton.

"How do you do," Hatton said.

"Maybe you'd like to tie him to a chair," O'Toole suggested. Hayes tossed Hatton the length of rope he'd gotten from the curtain and pushed the man into a chair. Hatton tied him up.

Nanos was looking out the window. "They're all just standing there."

O'Toole joined him there. "I don't know," he said. "If they're anything like this one, I don't think we have to worry about them coming in here."

"Does this one know where Wolenski is?" Billy Two asked.

"Who's Wolenski?" Hatton asked.

O'Toole gave Hayes a look and he hurriedly explained to Hatton what they'd found out from George.

O'Toole answered Billy's question. "He says all they have is a phone number.

"Do you believe him?" the big Osage asked.

"Yes."

"Why?" Hatton asked.

"Because I wouldn't trust him with my location, either, if he worked for me."

"If we had some help we could trace the phone number," Jessup suggested.

"We may not have to," O'Toole said. "If our friend the arm doctor knows who Wolenski is he may be able to lead us to him. Which reminds me." He picked up the telephone. "I'll have to tell the front desk to switch any calls to this room."

"What do we do now?" Erika asked. She had been sitting quietly, listening to the explanations, but had appeared, to Lee at least, to be getting gradually more agitated.

"We wait," Nanos answered flatly.

"That's all we've *been* doing," she wailed. There was a hysterical tone to her voice, which Hatton had been expecting. "Can't we take some kind of action? Nile could be anywhere by now!"

"Maybe we'll find out something tonight that will help us, Erika," Hatton said, her own tone soothing. "Then we can start moving."

They all hoped it would be true.

No lunch.

Barrabas had resigned himself to that fact, and was now anticipating dinner. He hoped that this time she would bring something to drink, as well. Granted, the fruit had been juicy—for that matter, so had the kisses—but he had been having visions of a large glass of icy-cold water.

Barrabas thought he knew how guinea pigs in a sensory deprivation experiment must feel, and he had only been deprived of sight, touch and taste. He was still able to use his nose and his ears on his environment, but they had already told him everything they could.

He reviewed the sum of his knowledge. He was in a cellar somewhere near the sea. Above him lived a man and a woman. Apparently they were lovers, but the woman was not completely satisfied with the arrangement. The woman was tall, not old, had long hair, full lips and a gentle touch. She wore an exotic perfume he'd never before smelled.

He knew nothing about the man—and that was what he needed to know, more than anything else.

Who the hell was the man?

JOSHUA WAITED while the boat docked and the men disembarked. There were six of them. More than enough, he thought. Individually, they were formidable. When he got through whipping them into shape as a team, they would be an unbeatable fighting force.

THE CALL CAME just after dark.

"All right," Jimmy Kontiza said, "we can do business."

"Where?" O'Toole asked.

"The same place."

"It's closed this late, isn't it?"

"All the better," Kontiza said. "In one hour."

O'Toole hung up.

"Was that him?" Jessup asked.

"Yes. The meet is set."

"What about them?" Nanos asked, looking out the window at Wolenski's hirelings.

O'Toole rubbed his jaw. "By now they may have gotten smart and put someone on the back," he said finally. "We're going to have to take them out."

"Permanently," Billy Two asked.

"That'll be up to them," O'Toole said. "Alex and I will go to the meet. The rest of you will have to take care of the tails."

"And me?" Erika asked.

O'Toole turned and faced her. "I'm sorry, Erika. You'll have to stay here with Mr. Jessup. We don't want to risk losing you, too."

If they did, Barrabas would never forgive them.

Hatton put her hand on Erika's shoulder and told her, "We'll be back soon."

Erika didn't answer. She put her head down, folded her arms and walked as far away from the rest of them as she could get in the small room.

"Billy," O'Toole said, "you'll have to go out ahead of us without being seen. If a tail falls in behind us, take him."

"Right. What about this one?" He nodded toward George, who was still tied to a chair.

"He's all right for now. Worry about the others."

"All right."

O'Toole's glance took in Billy Two, Claude Hayes and Lee Hatton. "After Billy stops anyone who tries to follow Nanos and me, go across the street and take care of the rest of them. Maybe it's time we showed these bastards we're not playing games anymore."

6

Barrabas heard the footsteps and his heartbeat quickened. He wasn't sure whether it was because of the woman, or because of what she might be bringing—some real food and drink. Worse than his hunger was his great thirst.

The door opened and closed, and she approached him. He knew it was she because he could smell her perfume.

Her gentle hands undid the gag and he tried to wet his lips with his dry tongue.

"Here is some water." She held the glass to his mouth and he drank greedily. "I have more, but first let me give you some food."

He opened his mouth and she put a piece of meat into it. It was not hot, but it was the best thing he ever tasted.

"This is left over from dinner," she said. "It's lamb."

Barrabas decided to risk trying to talk to her. "Did you cook it?"

He heard her sharp intake of breath, as if she were going to scold him for speaking. But she didn't. Then, after a moment, she said, "Yes, I prepared it."

"It's very good."

She put another piece into his mouth and said, "In your position, anything would taste good."

"Could I have some more water?"

"Yes."

She held the glass to his mouth and he drank, trying to control the elation he felt. She was having a conversation with him.

He was actually making some headway!

BILLY TWO HAD FOUND a window low enough for him to climb out, and positioned himself so that he could see the back door O'Toole and Nanos would be using. For the first time since their arrival in Greece—since Jessup had interrupted his sacred run in Oklahoma—Billy Two felt really alive. Every sense was heightened. The night felt and smelled different, and he could even see better.

Hawk Spirit was with him.

At 2:00 a.m. he saw O'Toole and Nanos leave the hotel by the service door at the back. The man watching the back of the hotel crossed the street and fell in behind the SOBs. Quickly, and quietly, Billy Two glided after him. Though the Indian had made no sound, the man sensed danger and whirled around, the knife in his hand stabbing toward Billy Two. But the Osage was faster, and the man's blood spilled quickly onto the ground.

A few minutes after that, Claude Hayes and Lee Hatton exited the hotel through the service door and found Billy Two waiting for them outside. Both of them were prepared for anything, though just how trouble would happen they didn't know.

There was a drop of blood on Billy Two's forearm that neither of them missed.

"Where is he?" Hayes asked, referring to Wolenski's watcher.

"In a dumpster out the back. He'll be collected with tomorrow's trash."

"Here," Hatton said, handing Billy Two a tissue. He wiped the drop of blood off his arm.

"Well, let's go around the front and settle things as best we can," Hayes said.

The six remaining tails were across the street from the hotel, but they were not clustered together. Still, the SOBs knew they would have to be quiet and quick. They weren't afraid of the men, who were supposed to be unarmed, but they didn't want to make an inordinate amount of noise—the last thing they needed was to get involved with the Athens police. But police or no police, the SOBs knew they had to take out Wolenski's clowns. And they did, though not quite the way it was intended. The men became suspicious, and violently so. The SOBs ended up dispatching a trio into the netherworld, but it hadn't been a happy experience—or a complete one.

Three down and three to go.

JOSHUA HAD DECIDED to make Dieter Muller his second in command.

Thirty-eight years old, Muller was German, six foot three and heavy through the chest and shoulders. He'd been a Green Beret in Vietnam, much decorated, and was in demand as a mercenary all over the world.

Large as Muller was, he was dwarfed by Angus McFadden. The big Scot was six-eight if he was an inch, and weighed close to three hundred pounds. He was the most powerful man Joshua had ever known. He was thirty-five.

The other four men were good, solid professionals: Sam Bowen, age twenty-nine; Elmore Kirk, age forty-one; Marcel DuLac, age forty; and Jeff "Handy" Hyde. At fifty-three, Handy Hyde was the oldest of the crew, but the most experienced. Hyde would have been Joshua's second choice as his exec.

Joshua explained the details of the situation to Muller. "You and the men will have to sleep outside. There's no room in the house."

"For the right amount of money we'd sleep in trees," Muller said.

"There's plenty of money in it, Dieter."

"That's why we're here . . . Joshua." Dieter Muller knew Joshua's real name, as did three of the others, but they had all been instructed not to use it. Joshua did not want Barrabas accidentally hearing his real name—not until he himself was ready to reveal it.

"Is it true?" Muller asked.

"What?"

"You have Barrabas?"

"I have him."

Muller shook his head. "You play a dangerous game, my friend. You should kill him at once."

"I am in charge, Dieter," Joshua said tightly.

"I don't dispute that," Muller said. "Of course you're in charge, but Barrabas may well be the most lethal man alive."

"Are you telling me you're afraid of him?"

"I respect his ability," was Muller's reply.

Joshua continued to outline the conditions of employment to Muller, who would relay the information to the other men.

"They understand that you are second in command?"

"They understand."

Joshua had contacted Muller first of all, and he had told the big German who else he wanted on the team. It had been Muller's job to contact and hire them.

"Any trouble with any of them?" Joshua inquired.

"None," Muller said. "They all know you, or rather, know *of* you. Do you want to speak to them?"

"For now I will speak only to you," Joshua said. "I can get acquainted with the others later."

"You're the boss."

"Yes," Joshua said, "I am."

Joshua might be the boss, Dieter Muller thought, but in Muller's opinion Joshua was making the wrong decision where Nile Barrabas was concerned.

Dead wrong.

NANOS AND O'TOOLE knew where they were going this time, so their trip to the museum was much shorter than the first time. Both the museum and the area around it were dark. There were iron bars over the doors and windows.

In front of the café where they'd had ouzo with Demetrius, they found him again, sitting at a table.

"We have business to discuss," Kontiza said. "Please, sit, and we can get started."

O'Toole and Nanos slipped into the two empty chairs that were waiting for them. When they found out what Kontiza had to offer they were disappointed.

"This is not good enough," O'Toole said to the arms dealer.

"I am doing the best I can," Kontiza said. "I recently filled a large order. If you could wait longer—"

"We can't wait," Nanos said.

"Then make your choice."

O'Toole and Nanos exchanged glances, and then O'Toole said, "Excuse us for a moment." They rose and walked a short distance from Kontiza, so he couldn't overhear their discussion.

"What do you think?" O'Toole said.

"We could take three Uzis and three Heckler & Koch pistols," Nanos said.

"Or we could take the AK-47s."

Nanos made a face. "Better the Uzis. I wish we knew what conditions we'd be working under."

"I wish he had the Berettas," O'Toole said.

"So do I. We're just going to have to mix and match, Liam. It's the best we can do."

"Yeah, I guess you're right."

"Let's take three Uzis, two H&Ks, and a Magnum for Billy Two. He likes them."

"I think we'd better take a pair of Starlite night-vision binoculars," O'Toole added. "Like you said, we don't know what the conditions are going to be."

"Agreed."

"All right," O'Toole said. "Let's go and place our order for six instruments of death."

AS SOON AS HATTON stepped on it she knew she was in trouble.

A tourist had been eating peanuts and had left shells lying on the sidewalk. When she stepped on one, it crunched. The man she was stalking turned and saw her, and reacted instantly. To her surprise—for the first man she'd taken on was unarmed—he whipped out a gun.

"Jesus," she said. She launched herself at him. He was almost double her weight, but was caught off balance when she barreled into him. They both hit the ground heavily. Hatton twisted around, trying to find an opening to use her knife. She finally stabbed at him with all her strength. The blade struck his leather belt and snapped in two.

He stiff-armed her then, shoving her away from him hard. She staggered and fell onto her back. The man sprang to his feet and aimed his gun at her. She closed her eyes.

No shot was fired. She heard the wet sound of a knife punching through his flesh. When she opened her eyes, a torrent of blood gushed from the man's mouth. He dropped the gun from nerveless fingers, then collapsed facedown. Had she not rolled swiftly out of the way, he would have crushed her beneath him.

Standing behind the fallen man was Billy Two. His huge Bowie knife had penetrated the man's back. In his left hand he held another dead man by the collar. He now released his grip so that the corpse crumpled to the ground. Then he stretched out his hand to Hatton and helped her to her feet.

"Thanks," she said.

"Don't mention it."

"Everything here all right?" Claude Hayes asked, coming up next to them.

"Yes," Hatton said. "The last one?"

"Done."

"What do we do with them?"

"We could put them where I put the other one, out the back," Billy Two suggested. "There's plenty of room."

"We'll have to make sure the coast is clear before we cart them all the way around the hotel," Hayes said. "We don't want to be seen."

"That isn't going to be easy," Lee Hatton said. "We'll have to make several trips."

"Just two trips." The big Osage picked up two men at a time. Hayes only managed one.

"All right, two trips," Hatton conceded. "As soon as someone sees us, though, we're in trouble."

"Hawk Spirit will be with us," Billy Two stated seriously.

"Well, in that case..." Claude Hayes exchanged a look with Hatton, then crossed the street toward the hotel, the dead man slung across his shoulder.

"EXCELLENT," Jimmy Kontiza said, rising from his chair. He put his hand out to shake with O'Toole. "I'm glad I was able to accommodate you."

"I'm sure your friend Gunther will be pleased," O'Toole said wryly, accepting the handshake. "After all, we only had to settle for—"

"I explained that if I had more time—"

"Or if we had more money," Nanos said, cutting the man off.

"That is not fair—"

"O'Toole interrupted, for something had occurred to him. "We need one other thing."

"What is that?" Kontiza asked.

"We do?" Nanos said.

"A P-38," O'Toole explained. Nanos nodded. The P-38 was Barrabas's favorite gun. Wherever he was, it was highly unlikely he was still carrying his own.

"I have one," Kontiza said, "but it will cost—"

"Throw it in," Nanos suggested. "It's the least you can do."

Kontiza stared at Nanos and O'Toole, then smiled and shook hands with Nanos.

"Yes, it is the least I can do."

But that night's business deal wasn't over yet. Besides weapons, the SOBs needed information if they were to succeed in finding and freeing Nile Barrabas.

"Before we leave," O'Toole said to Kontiza, "there's something else you might be able to help us with."

"Another gun?"

"No, not a gun," O'Toole said, "information."

Kontiza narrowed his eyes. "What kind of information?"

"Do you know a man named Wolenski? Stanley Wolenski?" O'Toole wondered why it was so difficult to take seriously a man with a name like Stanley Wolenski.

When Kontiza made a face, O'Toole knew that Wolenski was no stranger to the arms dealer.

"The man is like a wart on my ass," Kontiza said. "Always there, difficult to get rid of."

"Well, maybe we can remove it for you," O'Toole said. "That is, if you can tell us where we can find him."

"You must understand that even though the man is both a competitor and a loathsome lowlife," Kontiza said, "I would not tell you if you were not friends of Gunther Dykstra's."

"Yeah, we've seen how much Gunther's friendship means to you," Nanos said with sarcasm.

Kontiza frowned. "Since you feel that I have not treated you fairly in the matter of the arms, I will help you find Wolenski. Tomorrow night I will send a van to pick you up at your hotel. Your weapons will be in the van, and the driver will take you to Wolenski. More than that I cannot possibly do."

"Sure you can," O'Toole said.

Kontiza looked puzzled. "What do you mean?"

"You could do it tonight."

"Tonight?" Kontiza said. "That is impossible."

"For a friend of Gunther Dykstra?" O'Toole prodded. "Nothing is impossible."

Kontiza stroked his jaw thoughtfully and then gave a grudging smile. "This morning, then," he said. "At 5:00 a.m., while it's still dark. You will be ready?"

"We'll be waiting behind the hotel," O'Toole said.

"You must be there precisely at five, or my man will leave."

"Understood," Nanos said.

"And you must have the money."

"I have the money now—" O'Toole began, but Kontiza waved him away.

"Later will be soon enough. Cash on delivery—that is for the friends of Gunther Dykstra."

HOURS LATER Barrabas could still taste the lamb. The meat, combined with the water to assuage his thirst, had made him feel much better.

He was also encouraged by the conversation he'd had with the woman. He had been careful not to ask her name, or the name of her lover, because he didn't want to spook her. They had engaged in small talk, a mundane, essentially pointless conversation. Finally she had apologized to him for having to gag him again.

"That's all right," he said. "I understand. I just wish you'd take off the blindfold so I could see you."

There was a pause and then she said, "I...cannot do that."

"I know."

He felt her hands start to lift the gag from around his neck to his mouth and he asked quickly, "Will you be coming back again?"

Again there was some hesitation before she answered. "I—I do not know. I will try."

"I hope you do," he said just as she lifted the gag into place.

Before she left the room she surprised Barrabas by placing a tender kiss on his forehead.

As she walked out he couldn't help but feel he was making some progress.

But toward what?

O'TOOLE AND NANOS returned to Jessup's room at 3:50 a.m.

"Seventy minutes from now," O'Toole told the others, "we'll have our guns, as well as transportation to Stanley Wolenski."

"Why?" Jessup asked.

"Why what?"

"Why is our friend being so damned helpful?"

"Maybe Erika can tell us that," O'Toole suggested. "Erika, what did Gunther say about Kontiza?"

"Just that he owed my brother a lot," Erika replied. "I don't know the details."

"Well, apparently the debt is a heavy one," O'Toole said. "He couldn't offer us much of a selection on guns, so he's making it up to us this way."

"So you trust him?" Jessup asked.

O'Toole took a moment before answering. The only people in the world he trusted were in this room—them and Barrabas. To trust anyone else was to place his life in the hands of people who couldn't carry it.

"No, I don't trust him," he finally said, "but I don't have any reason to distrust him, either."

"What are the arrangements?" Claude Hayes asked.

O'Toole explained that a van would be out back at 5:00 a.m., and not only to deliver their weapons, but to pick up and deliver the SOBs directly to Stanley Wolenski's doorstep.

"I hope that's truly the case," Jessup said skeptically. "I hope the van will deliver you to Wolenski's doorstep, and not into Wolenski's hands."

7

At 4:55 a.m., Liam O'Toole, Alex Nanos, William Starfoot II, Claude Hayes and Dr. Leona Hatton were standing behind the hotel, just outside the service door. Walker Jessup and Erika Dykstra had remained in her suite, along with George, the first man they'd captured, who had been trussed up and deposited in a closet. They'd intended to put him in the bathtub, but Erika pointed out that she might have to use the facilities, and didn't relish having an audience.

O'Toole checked the luminous hands of his watch and announced, "Four fifty-six. Four minutes to go."

"About what Jessup said . . ." Lee Hatton began.

"Which time?" Nanos asked.

"When he asked how we can be sure we're not being delivered into some kind of a trap."

"We can't," O'Toole said, "but this is the only lead we have to the colonel and I think we have to follow it up. Anybody who disagrees, say so now."

"It's not that I disagree," Hatton's tone was defensive.

"I understand how you feel, Lee," O'Toole said. "We all feel that way. But if Gunther Dykstra vouches for the man, then I think the odds are good that we'll get what we want from him, and won't be betrayed.

"It'll be light in half an hour," Billy Two announced.

"Doesn't Hawk Spirit come out in the daylight?" Nanos asked.

"Don't scoff," Billy Two said, not looking at the Greek.

"I'm just asking—" Nanos started to answer, but he stopped when a van turned into the street, its lights on high beam.

"This is it!" O'Toole said.

Billy Two put his hand on the hilt of his knife. Claude Hayes had the Browning he'd taken from one of the men he killed and he held it in his hand, hanging down beside his leg. Hatton had the gun that her enemy had almost used on her, a Colt Woodsman .22. Apparently he had fancied himself a sharpshooter.

The van, a new one, painted a metallic blue, pulled up to the curb and the sliding door on their side opened.

"Let's go." O'Toole led the way across the sidewalk to the van.

He got in first and the others piled in after him. The driver was the only man inside. He'd left the wheel to open the door, and now climbed back into his seat. Claude Hayes sat right behind the driver and beside Lee Hatton.

Billy Two slid the door shut.

"You know where we want to go?" O'Toole asked the driver.

"Yes," he said.

"And our merchandise?"

"Underneath the tarp." The man turned the wheel, pulling the van away from the curb.

O'Toole tugged back a corner of the tarpaulin and saw a crate underneath. With Billy Two's knife he pried off the top, then hauled out the weaponry, handing one piece to each of them. The Uzis were actually Mini-Uzis, just as lethal but easily concealed.

"Here," He said, handing the Magnum to Billy Two.

Everyone busied themselves checking out the action on the weapons they were holding. One by one they nodded to O'Toole, indicating that the guns looked fine.

"I wish we had a chance to test-fire them," Nanos said.

"We may get that chance soon enough," O'Toole said. He tucked an H&K pistol into his belt, something he didn't like to do, but they hadn't asked for holsters, and hadn't been supplied with any. He picked up the P-38 and put it into his jacket pocket.

"How far?" he asked the driver.

"Ten minutes."

"Will he be alone?"

"I doubt it."

"Any idea how many men he keeps around him?"

The man shrugged. "Depends on how safe he feels."

"Well," O'Toole said to everyone, "let's hope he feels real safe, this morning."

STANLEY WOLENSKI LAY AWAKE in bed. He hadn't heard from his men and that worried him. He wasn't worried enough to bother Joshua this early, though. He'd decided that if he didn't hear from them by eight a.m. he'd contact Joshua for further instructions.

Wolenski lived in a house by the sea, only five miles from the Acropolis. Outside the house he had six men stationed, and three more inside. They were armed with Berettas and AK-47s.

Now he was wondering whether he needed more than nine guards.

He rolled over and turned on his bedside lamp. He opened the top drawer of the nightstand, touched the .45 he kept there, then closed the drawer.

He left the light on.

JOSHUA AWOKE at five a.m., listening to the breathing of the woman beside him. At six he'd rise and talk to Dieter Muller about the drills he wanted him to run with the men.

By now the SOBs must have found out Wolenski's name, if they didn't already have Wolenski himself. Joshua figured that the little man, as loathsome as he was, would probably hold out for a whole day before revealing to them where Joshua was. It would take them another day to work their way through the meager defenses Joshua had set up as a front. Two days, maybe two and a half, and they'd be here.

It wasn't long, but Muller and the others would have jelled by then, because they were pros. They knew every aspect of fighting there was to know. All they had to do now was learn about one another, and how to work together. Their other advantage would be that they knew the island, and the Soldiers of Barrabas did not. These plus factors would have to offset the fact that the SOBs had been working together as a team for a long time.

The main disadvantage to the SOBs, however, was the fact that he had deprived them of their leader. Joshua's men, with him leading them, were certain to come out victorious.

After he had killed all of Colonel Nile Barrabas's SOBs, he would reveal himself to Barrabas. He'd stand in front of the bodies of the SOBs, piled one on top of the other, and have the woman remove Barrabas's blindfold.

Barrabas would see his conqueror against the backdrop of his own people's corpses.

THE VAN CAME TO A STOP. They were on a road by the sea, with no houses in sight.

"Why are we stopping here?" O'Toole asked.

"Wolenski's house is around that bend," the driver replied. "If I get any closer they'll hear you coming. You'd better get out here and walk."

The SOBs exchanged glances. What if they were being let off in the middle of nowhere?

"We'd like to check that out first," O'Toole said.

The man shrugged. "I was told you guys were careful."

O'Toole looked at Billy Two. "Check it out, Billy."

"Right." The Osage moved into the passenger seat and got out through that door, which was quieter to open than the sliding door.

"Is he an American Indian?" the driver inquired.

"That's right," Nanos said.

"I've never seen one before," the driver said, "except on television. He's a big one."

"And mean," Nanos told him. "If there's nothing around that bend, you'll soon find out how mean."

The man looked unconcerned.

Billy Two jogged around the bend and then off the road. He glided through some trees and finally came to a point where he could see a house. He decided to take a closer look before going back to the van. He soon spotted the six guards, all armed with what looked like AK-47s. He wondered how many men were inside the house.

Satisfied, he turned and worked his way back to the van. He slid into the passenger seat and closed the door quietly.

"The house is there."

"How many men?" O'Toole asked.

"Six, outside."

"Armed?"

"AK-47s."

"All right, troops," O'Toole said, "it's show time."

They all got out through the passenger door, O'Toole going last. He counted out a roll of paper money to pay for the weapons. The driver took the cash and shoved it in his pocket.

"You're not going to count it?"

"I was told to trust you."

"That's nice to know." O'Toole turned to follow the others.

The driver stopped him, asking in a whisper, "You know, about that Indian?"

"Yeah?"

"What kind is he?"

"Osage."

"The ones I've seen on TV were Apaches, I think," the driver said.

"That's not the same thing."

The man shrugged. "Good luck," he said.

"Thanks." O'Toole trotted up the road after the others as the van made a U-turn and drove off.

The sky was starting to brighten.

O'Toole asked Billy to lead the way. Billy took them through the trees to the edge of the property. From there they could see three of the men.

"The other three are on the other side," Billy said.

"How long will it take," O'Toole asked, "for you, Claude and Alex to work your way around?"

"Three minutes."

"Take five."

"Right."

"Did you get a look inside?"

"I didn't get that close."

"There are bound to be more men inside, plus Wolenski himself," O'Toole said. "If they hear shooting they'll probably stay inside and wait for us."

"They'll hear shooting, all right," Nanos said. "This isn't going to be easy."

"Everybody got your extra ammo?" O'Toole asked.

"What there was of it," Nanos said, referring to the scanty supplies the weapons merchant had sold them.

"Well, there are more guns waiting for us right over there," O'Toole reminded him. "This is a pretty isolated area, so let's not be shy about taking them."

They all nodded.

"Wouldn't it be funny if the Colonel was in there?" Alex Nanos said.

"Funny," O'Toole said, "but not bloody likely."

O'Toole and Hatton gave the other three the full five minutes to work their way around them.

"You ready?" O'Toole asked. He held his H&K in his right hand.

"As ready as I'll ever be." Hatton was holding one of the Uzis, and had the Woodsman in her belt.

"Come on."

O'Toole moved through the trees silently, stepping onto the property. Hatton was right behind him.

FROM WHERE THEY STOOD Billy Two, Hayes and Nanos could see the other three guards.

"They're not following any kind of pattern," Nanos said. "They're just milling about." He was holding an Uzi, and had an H&K in his belt.

"They're smoking and laughing," Hayes observed. "This might be easier than we thought." He, too, was armed with an Uzi, and had the Browning in his jacket pocket.

"And it might not." Billy Two's big right hand dwarfed the Magnum it was wrapped around.

"Let's fan out," Hayes suggested. "We each take the man nearest to us."

The other two nodded, and slipped out of cover to close in on Wolenski's guards.

Billy Two got right up to his man, who was standing on the patio, before the guard knew what was happening. At such close quarters the Osage preferred his Bowie knife to the Magnum. He pushed the gun under his belt and drove the knife into the man's back to the hilt. As the sentry's hand started to tighten convulsively around his AK-47, Billy Two ripped it from his grasp.

At that moment a spotlight came on, bathing the patio in bright white light. A man opened the sliding door from the house and stepped out. He was shirtless, an AK-47 in his hands.

"You guys want a break—" he started to say, and then saw Billy Two. "Jesus!"

He tried to bring the AK-47 around, but Billy Two was faster. The blast from his Magnum riddled the man with bullets and broke the glass of the sliding door behind him.

Then all hell broke loose.

8

Stanley Wolenski heard the shots and leaped from his bed. His right foot caught in the sheet and he fell, striking his head a painful blow on the wooden floor. He lay there for a moment, stunned, then pulled himself together and clawed the .45 from the night table drawer.

Outside the house, Liam O'Toole heard the Magnum shots and raised his H&K. The sentry he'd been stalking had turned toward the house at the sound of the shots. O'Toole fired, sending a round into the back of his skull.

Hatton's target was a guard who was reclining against a tree. At the sound of the shots the man automatically dropped into a crouch. The single shot from O'Toole's pistol, which followed, caused him to look around. He spotted Hatton.

He squeezed the trigger of his AK-47 before bringing it to bear on her. The rounds cuts some trees and bushes to ribbons, giving Hatton time to fire her Uzi. Already off balance, the man spun, then sprawled on the ground. Hatton quickly checked him to make sure he was dead and ran to the house.

Inside, Wolenski ran from his bedroom, his head throbbing. He found his three men in the dining room.

"Get out there! Get out there!" he shouted.

"Sir, we're better off waiting for them to try and come in—" one of them started.

But Wolenski, panicked, had cut him off. "I don't want them inside, damn it! Go out there and get them!"

The three exchanged glances and shrugged, then moved toward the ruined sliding door.

On the far side of the house, where Billy Two had launched the attack, Claude Hayes and Alex Nanos began firing their Uzis as soon as the sentries turned their attention toward Billy Two.

The Osage presented a tempting target, bathed in the spotlight that had just been turned on. He shot out the spotlight with one blast of his Magnum, then hit the deck.

Hayes's burst caught one man at the knees, knocking him down. Somehow the man held on to his weapon and fired it. His wild shots cut through the air, some of them smashing the windows of the house, others chewing up the patio. Some of the stone chips it sent flying hit Billy Two on the right forearm, but the big Osage held on to his Magnum.

Nanos's target took two rounds through the neck. Blood gushed from his wounds as he crumpled to the ground, landing on top of his weapon.

At that moment three men barreled out of the house, shouting and firing their AK-47s. By then O'Toole, Hatton, Hayes and Nanos had reached the patio, where Billy Two was already lying low. All five SOBs opened fire at the same time, and Wolenski's three inside men were torn apart by a hail of flying lead.

In the silence that followed O'Toole shouted, "Count 'em up."

"Two here," Billy Two shouted.

"Three," Nanos said.

"I've got number four," Hatton called out.

"Five here," O'Toole put in, "and three from inside makes eight."

"I got one at the knees," Hayes added. He stood over the man and kicked the gun from his hands, then bent over and relieved him of his Beretta. Pain was etched on the wounded man's face, and his eyes were glazed. "He's secured."

"That gives us nine," O'Toole said. "How many came from inside?"

"Three," Billy Two said.

"So that's everyone we've come across so far," O'Toole said. "Billy, give it the once-over out here while we move in."

The big Osage melted into the trees.

O'Toole and Hatton joined Hayes and Nanos on the patio.

"How bad?" O'Toole asked Hayes, looking down at the injured man.

"He won't last five minutes."

O'Toole looked at the house. "We don't know how many are inside."

"We don't even know if Wolenski is inside," Hayes said.

"Claude, take the back, Lee the right, Alex the left. I'll go in this way in one minute."

"Luck," Nanos said, and trotted around the house. Hatton moved swiftly to the right. Hayes went with her and kept on going till he reached the back.

O'Toole counted sixty, and leaped through the smashed patio door.

Inside the house Wolenski was in a panic. He held the .45 so tight that his hand hurt. The shooting outside had stopped. He'd had nine men out there, but he had no way of knowing how many they'd been facing. All he knew was that the shooting had stopped, and someone had won.

"Pappas?" he called out. There was no answer. "Demas?" He called out the names of all nine men. Not one answered.

Suddenly he thought he would piss his pants. He crouched behind a chair in the living room. "Jesus . . . Jesus . . ." he moaned.

Was somebody trying to move in on his territory, he wondered, or was this a result of the work he was doing for Joshua?

He thought about his strange instructions from Joshua—that his men be unarmed and not try to hide the fact that they were working a tail job. Even stranger, the instructions to do nothing when they turned up missing.

Wait, Joshua had said, just wait.

The son of a bitch with the scarred face had set him up!

While Wolenski was wondering what Joshua's game really was, O'Toole dived through the ruined sliding door, landed rolling and came to a stop by the dining room table, which had been torn up by stray bullets. He upended the table and took refuge behind it.

Outside, the sun had risen and now light came streaming in through the broken glass. He looked around the room, which had been chewed to pieces, and saw no one. Was Wolenski alone, hiding somewhere in the house, he wondered, or were there others still to be dealt with?

O'Toole fingered the AK-47 he'd picked up outside, then pushed against the table, sliding it ahead of him to the doorway.

Wolenski saw the movement in the dining room and fired once. His bullet took a piece out of the overturned table.

"Who are you?" he shouted. "What do you want?"

"We want to talk to you, Wolenski," O'Toole called back. "Drop your gun and come out. The house is surrounded."

"No good, no good!" Wolenski shouted. He fired twice more, each shot taking a huge piece out of the table.

At the back of the house Claude Hayes heard the shots and decided to go. He picked a window and hurled himself through it, landing in a shower of glass. He rolled until he hit something. A bed. He crawled on his knees to the bedroom doorway. He could hear Liam O'Toole's voice, and that of another man.

He peeked cautiously into the hall and then eased out into it. Carefully, his Uzi held ready, he worked his way down the hall. When he came to the end of it he found himself facing the living room. Crouched behind a chair, with his back to the hall, was a man holding a .45. Hayes figured it had to be Wolenski.

"Come on, Wolenski," O'Toole shouted, confirming Hayes's guess, "don't make this hard."

"Come and get it, you bastard!" Wolenski fired another round from the .45.

Hayes worked the cocking handle on the Uzi so that Wolenski could hear it. The man stiffened. "I'd do what he says if I was you, friend," Hayes told him.

"Shit," Wolenski said, freezing. "Fuck."

"Shit and fuck all you want," Hayes said, "but first we got some talking to do. Throw the gun away from you."

"Son of a *bitch*!" Wolenski screamed, and tossed the .45 aside.

O'Toole called Hatton and Nanos into the house, and was surprised when Billy Two accompanied them, amazed by how quick and skillful his friend was.

"Nothing?"

"It's very quiet," Billy said, "but you might want to ask him."

O'Toole turned to face Wolenski, who was standing up now, with Hayes behind him.

"How many men did you have, Stanley?" he asked.

Wolenski didn't answer right away. Hayes nudged him with the barrel of his Uzi.

"N-nine," Wolenski said, "I had nine." Bitterly, as much to himself as anyone, he said, "I knew I should have had more."

"More wouldn't have helped," Nanos said.

"Let's get some light in here," O'Toole said. The living room was on the west side, and the sun was still too low in the sky to disperse the shadows.

A couple of table lamps had caught some lead and were lying on the floor. Nanos picked one up and tried it. The bare bulb shone brightly, like a miniature sun.

O'Toole sent Nanos and Hayes to search the house. He then turned to Wolenski. "Sit down, Stanley. We have some questions."

"I'm not answering any questions," Wolenski said as he sank heavily into an armchair.

"What are you into these days, Stanley?" O'Toole asked. "You're supposed to be a second-class arms dealer—"

"Second class!" Wolenski snorted. "Have you looked at what you're carrying?"

"I have," O'Toole replied, "and we appreciate your men supplying us with their Berettas. But right now I want *you* to supply me with a few answers. If you don't, I'm going to have my big friend here take off a few strips of your hide...slowly."

Billy Two took out his knife and smiled at Wolenski, who shuddered.

"Why were your men tailing us?" O'Toole asked.

"Because I told them to."

"That's funny, Stanley. But who told you to have them tail us?"

"A client."

"Now we're getting someplace," O'Toole said. "Who is the client?"

"He's a big client. If I rat on him I'll lose his business."

"Where are you from, Stanley?" O'Toole asked. "Originally?"

"New York."

"Brooklyn?"

"How'd you know?"

"A lucky guess. How come you're not plying your trade back in Brooklyn?"

"Nobody wants to stay in Brooklyn," Wolenski said.

O'Toole had seen something flash into Wolenski's eyes before the man effectively masked it and answered. He decided to play a hunch.

"I beg to differ. I know a lot of people from Brooklyn, and they all like it."

"The only people who like Brooklyn are—" Wolenski broke off abruptly.

"Are who, Stanley?"

"People who were born there," Wolenski said. But O'Toole was convinced that wasn't what he originally intended to say.

Lee Hatton was watching O'Toole closely, wondering what he was getting at. Billy Two was keeping his eyes on Stanley Wolenski.

"Let me take a wild guess here, Stanley." O'Toole gazed up toward the ceiling. "Um, you left Brooklyn in particular, and New York in general, because you fell out of favor."

"Bad guess."

"Is it? It strikes me that a guy like you would be into a lot of things in Brooklyn, all of them on a shoestring. You got somebody mad at you, didn't you, Stanley? Otherwise why would a nice Jewish boy like you from Brooklyn be plying his dubious trade in Greece?"

"I like the food."

"That's another thing," O'Toole said. "How could a nice Brooklyn boy stand to be this far from pizza?"

"I don't like pizza," Wolenski said. "In fact, I don't like Italian food. In fact—" He stopped short again, as if he had been about to give something away.

"You don't like Italians, am I right, Stanley?"

Wolenski didn't answer.

Billy Two looked at O'Toole, who shook his head. O'Toole thought he had the situation well in hand, all because he knew a Brooklyn accent when he heard one.

"And they don't like you," he went on.

Nanos and Hayes reentered the room and Hatton waved at them to keep silent.

"You got in trouble with wise guys in Brooklyn, didn't you, Stanley?" O'Toole asked.

No answer.

"And you left New York to get away from them, but they've got long arms, so you ended up leaving the United States and coming to Greece. Oh, there may have been a few stops along the way, but you ended up here, making your living the same way, doing nickel-and-dime jobs."

"Nickel-and-dime!" Wolenski said, offended. "You don't know what you're talking about!"

"Sure I do. Why, I'll bet if I place a few calls to some friends in Brooklyn—like in Bensonhurst or Sheeps-head Bay—I might find somebody who'd pay a lot to find out where you are these days."

Wolenski's eyes began darting all over the room, looking for a way out.

"You—you can't."

"Sure I can. I'll even use your phone so the call goes on your bill."

O'Toole reached for the phone and Wolenski said, "Wait! Wait a minute!"

"All right, Stanley." O'Toole took his hand away from the phone. "You've got a minute, but make the most of it. It's the only one you're going to get.

"Jesus!" Wolenski said, running his hand through his thinning hair. He was sweating profusely and they could all smell his fear.

What Wolenski was trying to figure out was who he had more to fear from, Joshua or the pepperoni eaters back home. God, but he hated those wop bastards! And he feared them. First they had driven him from Brooklyn, then from New York, and finally from the country, all because of one mistake with the daughter of a Brooklyn don. Shit, she wanted to turn pro, he never forced her to turn tricks for him.

Still, the wops were back in the United States, and Joshua was here. Maybe these bastards could get at Joshua and take him right out of the picture. Then Wolenski would be safe from Joshua, and still out of reach of the wise guys in Brooklyn. Christ, he thought, I should have worked on ditching the Brooklyn accent.

"All right, all right," he said.

"All right what, Stanley?" O'Toole asked.

"My client's name is Joshua."

"Joshua what?"

"I don't know. That's what he wants to be called. Just Joshua."

"You're saying that's not his name?"

"I'd bet it's not, but I don't know what is. All I know is Joshua. There, you've got all I know."

"Oh, I doubt that," O'Toole said. "Don't try to kid me, Stanley. How do you get in touch with Joshua? How does he get in touch with you? Where do you meet him?"

"Okay, okay," Wolenski admitted. "I got a radio inside, that's how we contact each other."

"What about seeing him?"

"He sends somebody here to get me."

"And to take you where?"

"I don't know."

"Stanley..."

"I'm not kidding," Wolenski said. "He sends a guy here to get me in a car, but I'm blindfolded before I even get in. They don't take off the blindfold until Joshua's standing right in front of me."

"Are you driven all the way there?" Lee Hatton asked.

Wolenski looked at Hatton quickly, and even though he was in a bad situation, looked her up and down once before answering. "No, they drive me to a boat, and we take a boat to an island, I guess."

"What island?" O'Toole asked.

"I don't know. I'm always blindfolded. I tole ya that!" His Brooklyn accent was becoming even more pronounced.

"All right," O'Toole said, "so we'll have to get on the horn and request a ride. When the guy gets here—"

"No more rides. It can't be done."

"What?"

"Joshua said I wasn't coming out to the island anymore. There wasn't any need."

"Well, you call him—"

"He won't send anyone, I tell ya. You don't know him. When he makes a decision, he don't change it."

Nanos looked at O'Toole. "There are thousands of islands..." he said.

"I know." O'Toole bit his bottom lip, thinking.

"You've got to give me something else, Stanley," he finally said.

"That's it. That's all I've got."

"No, it isn't," Hayes said. "You've seen this Joshua, right?"

"Sure."

"What's he look like?"

"Jesus, he's an ugly son of a bitch. More than half his face is covered by this ugly, shiny scar tissue."

O'Toole looked at the others. "We know anybody like that?"

The response from everyone was negative.

"I know a guy with a scar beside his right eye, but not half his face," Nanos said, shaking his head.

"Can you tell us anything else about Joshua?" O'Toole asked Wolenski.

"Just that aside from the scar the guy's almost perfect. He always wears a bathing suit, and he's built like a Greek god. Still, with his face like that I don't see how the broad with him can stand—"

"He's got a woman with him?" O'Toole said, leaping on that bit of information.

"Has he!" Wolenski said. "Only the highest priced hooker in Athens—"

"You've seen her? You know her?"

"I saw her once. She was looking out the window of this shack. I only caught a glimpse, but with a face like that it was enough."

"Do you know who she is?"

"Sure," Wolenski said, suddenly aware that he might have a way out.

"Well, who is she?" O'Toole asked.

"Er," Wolenski said, "we got to do a deal, first."

"We'll do a deal." O'Toole nodded to Billy Two.

The big Osage took hold of Wolenski's pajama top and bunched it up in his hand. He pulled the man closer to him and placed the blade of his knife alongside his jaw.

"My friend here is going to give you a shave," O'Toole explained, "only he's going to take off more than just whiskers. He's going to take about an inch of hide with it."

"Wait, wait!" Wolenski said, flapping his arms as if trying to fly.

"Talk, Stanley," O'Toole said. "A name and address will get you off the hook very nicely."

"Her name's Julianne," he said, "that's all I know. She's just about the highest-priced hooker in the city."

"And who do you see in Athens when you want the highest-priced hooker in town?" O'Toole asked.

"Only one man," Wolenski said. "His name is Kontiza. Demetrius Kontiza!"

O'Toole looked at the others. It was Nanos who shrugged and said, "What goes around comes around, doesn't it?"

Wolenski's car was a big, old Citroën. They tied him up and put him in the trunk. Then they loaded the car with as many guns as they could. With no large, corporate bankroll behind them, this time, they felt they could never have too many guns. It would be a novelty, having such a selection to choose from.

While they were doing all this they had a chance to discuss the events that had just taken place, and some of their implications.

"Why am I not surprised that we're going back to Kontiza?" O'Toole asked the others. It was just a rhetorical question.

"Do you think he sent us after Wolenski so we'd get him out of the way for him?" Nanos asked.

"I don't know." O'Toole scratched his head. "No, remember, we brought up Wolenski's name."

"So everything worked for him," Nanos said. "Coincidence. It's happened before."

"Besides," O'Toole added, "I don't think Kontiza is that threatened by Stanley Wolenski."

"And what about this Joshua guy with the scarred face?" Nanos asked. "Why would he hire a guy like Wolenski?"

"I can't answer that."

"And is he the one who has the colonel?"

"I can't answer that, either."

"I know you can't," Nanos returned irritably. "I'm just wondering."

"I know," O'Toole said. "So are we all."

"What are we going to do with him?" Hatton asked. Behind them Wolenski was banging on the trunk lid, shouting something muffled they couldn't understand.

"I'd kill him," O'Toole said, "except he might still be of some use to us."

"So?" Hatton asked.

"So...we take him back to the hotel and leave him with Jessup and Erika."

"That'll make them very happy," Claude Hayes said. "Especially as they're still baby-sitting George."

"I hope Erika wasn't expecting us to return with the colonel," Billy Two said.

"I don't think any of us were really expecting that yet, Billy," O'Toole said, "even though things have developed pretty fast overnight."

"Well, it's morning now," Nanos said as they all piled into the car. "A new day. Now we have to find Kontiza. How are we supposed to do that?"

O'Toole was behind the wheel. He smiled at Nanos and started the engine. "See? I told you we'd need Wolenski again."

He steered the car down the drive to the road, then turned and looked at the others. "Does anyone know how to get back to the fucking hotel?"

9

"I could have died in there!" Stanley Wolenski said for the third time in as many minutes.

They had gathered in Erika's suite again, where there was much more room for their swelling numbers than in single rooms.

"How's George?" O'Toole asked.

"Quiet," Jessup said. "Who's this?"

"This is Stanley Wolenski, the pride of Brooklyn," O'Toole answered. "The one in the closet works for him."

"And who does he work for?" Jessup asked.

"Joshua."

"Who the hell is Joshua?"

"A man who has a scarred face."

"Shit," Wolenski said, "he's got more scar than face. You got one of my men in the closet? Where are you gonna put me?"

"In the blasted commode if you don't shut up!" Nanos threatened.

"What about Nile?" Erika asked anxiously.

"It's a pretty sure bet that this Joshua has him, Erika," O'Toole said.

"And who is Joshua?" she asked.

"That's what we have to find out," Hatton said. "And where he is."

"And who can help us with that?" Jessup asked.

"Stanley can."

"Me?" Wolenski said. "I've told you everything I know already."

"Not everything," O'Toole said. "Do you know who told us where you live? Hell, he gave us a ride to your house."

"Who's the son of a bitch who ratted me out?"

"Kontiza. Demetrius Kontiza."

"Like hell!"

"He sold us these guns and sent us after you," O'Toole stated firmly.

"We ain't friends, but he wouldn't rat." But Wolenski was beginning to look uncertain.

"You're not a friend of Jimmy, huh?" O'Toole asked.

"How'd you know he's called— Wait a minute. Is this on the level?"

"On the level," O'Toole said.

"Son of a bitch! That *scumbag*!"

"Now it's your turn," O'Toole said. "We want to talk to Kontiza, and we don't want to go through channels."

"Let me drive," Wolenski said eagerly. "I'll take you right to him, just let me drive!"

O'Toole looked at the others. They nodded. To all of them Wolenski's anger sounded sincere.

"All right, Stanley," O'Toole said, "you're going to get your chance for revenge."

"Let's go—"

"Wait a minute." O'Toole grabbed his arm and put his forefinger right into the smaller man's face. "I'm going to tell you this so that even you can understand it. If you fuck with us, your ass is in a sling! You got that?"

"I got it," Wolenski said, glancing at Billy Two, who, to him, was the most impressive of the lot. "I got it!"

"Now let's go," O'Toole said.

A few hours later, after they had driven all around the city and made at least half a dozen stops, O'Toole told Wolenski to pull over.

"He'll be at this next place, I'm sure."

"Pull the fuck over!" O'Toole shouted.

Wolenski pulled over and stopped the car so abruptly they were all thrown forward.

"You're jerking us around, Stanley."

"I'm not."

"You said you knew where Kontiza would be."

"I know a few places he *could* be."

"That isn't what you said. You've made us waste time we can't afford to waste, Stanley. We're very angry with you."

"Wait, wait!" Wolenski sneaked a look at Billy Two in the rearview mirror. "I just remembered how we can find him."

"Stanley—"

"I swear! Just listen."

"All right," O'Toole said, "we're listening."

"When I need a girl—I mean a real knockout for a client—I get her from Kontiza."

"Stanley," Lee Hatton said reproachfully. She was seated in the front between Wolenski and O'Toole. "You're a pimp, too."

"Not really," Stanley explained, "but once in a while I do a favor for some big clients, you know?"

"And you throw the business Kontiza's way?" O'Toole sounded skeptical. "He's your competitor."

"He's got the gash, if you know what I mean," Wolenski said. He then looked at Hatton and said, "Excuse my French, lady."

"Don't worry about it," Hatton said.

"So what are you suggesting?" O'Toole kept at the man.

"Let's go back to the hotel," Wolenski proposed. "I'll make a few calls and we'll have Kontiza there to see you in nothing flat."

O'Toole turned around in his seat and looked at the others.

"Anybody got any better ideas?"

"I've got one," Billy Two volunteered, "but only if this one doesn't work."

In the rearview mirror Wolenski could see that Billy Two was looking right at him.

"This'll work, friend," Wolenski said hastily. "Believe me, this will work."

"Your track record is not exactly great, Stanley," O'Toole reminded him. "All right, get this thing back to the hotel. We've wasted enough time already."

THEY HAD WOLENSKI.

Joshua was sure they had Wolenski; otherwise, he thought, he would have heard from the little Jew by now.

So, if they had him, then things were moving along right on schedule.

Good.

Joshua was standing on a huge rock behind his house. He watched as Dieter Muller worked the men. From this distance the men couldn't make out his face, and even if they could have, would they have recognized him?

He thought not.

That morning he had asked Julianne if she would mind continuing to feed Barrabas his meager meals.

"If that's what you want," she answered.

His reason was simple: Muller had been adamant that morning that Joshua should kill Barrabas.

"The potential for danger is too great when you're dealing with him," Muller had said. "You've got to kill him, Joshua, or let me do it."

"No," Joshua had said.

"Then let one of my—"

"No! That's final, Muller."

Muller had stared at him and then looked away. Joshua knew the man was not averting his eyes from fear, but because looking at the scarred face made him uncomfortable. Sometimes—not often—Joshua's disfigurement worked to his advantage.

After that discussion he was convinced that if he let Muller or any of the other men near Barrabas to feed him, they might kill him, and he was not ready for Barrabas to die. So he had asked Julianne to carry on, and she had agreed.

How could she not?

After all, she was bought and paid for.

JULIANNE BROUGHT Barrabas an omelet and fruit for breakfast. She'd pretended to prepare the eggs for herself, and when Joshua left the house to watch his men work she put them aside for Barrabas.

More and more, Julianne had become convinced that this man Barrabas was her only escape from Joshua.

If she could trust him.

Now Barrabas opened his mouth and she put another forkful of eggs inside. He chewed and swallowed, and thanked her again.

"Do not keep thanking me."

"I wish I knew your name," he said, "or that I could see you."

"I cannot remove the blindfold," she said, her tone apologetic.

Barrabas decided not to push that particular point just now.

"Your name, then?"

There was a long pause, then she started to say something. It sounded like Julie, but she had stopped short.

"Julie? Is that your name?"

No answer.

He decided to play a hunch. "No, a woman like you wouldn't be named Julie. More like . . . Julianne. Yes, that's a name that suits you more."

"How did—" she started, then stopped.

"I'm right, aren't I?"

"Yes."

"Julianne . . . take off my blindfold."

"I can't."

"Just for a moment."

He waited while she worked it out, and then her hands touched the blindfold and it was off.

At first he couldn't see anything, for he'd been blindfolded for days now. Everything was a blur. Luckily there were no windows in the room, just a light bulb overhead, and gradually his vision cleared. He took his first look at her.

She had long, dark hair, all right, although it was pulled behind her head now, worn close to her skull, and not flowing free, as he was sure it had sometimes been. Her cheekbones were high, her eyes slanted and beautiful. She was easily one of the loveliest women he'd ever seen in his life. She had a long graceful neck, a firm jaw, full lips...

"I have to put it back on," she said nervously.

"A moment more. Please."

She settled back, the blindfold held in her hands.

He looked around. He'd been right about his surroundings. He was in a cellar. Although there were no windows, he felt a draft from somewhere other than the door. The door itself was made of wood, and very heavy from the look of it.

"Where are we?" he asked.

"An island."

"What island?"

He could see the fear in her face. No longer did he think of her as some love-starved female who had formed a fixation for him. This woman would never be love starved. She had some other reason for kissing him, talking to him, feeding him....

"You need help, don't you?" he asked.

She didn't answer right away, then said, "Yes."

She was wearing a bikini, but he concentrated on not looking at her willowy body.

"I can help you," he said.

"I don't know. . . ."

"But first you have to help me."

"I'm. . . ."

"You're frightened, I know," he said.

"I have to go," she said. "Please. . ."

"Think about it, Julianne," he said. "We can help each other."

She stared at him for a moment, then leaned forward and kissed him, pressing her lips to his tightly.

"If you help me," she whispered, "I will be yours. . ."

She hurriedly replaced the blindfold and he heard her walk quickly from the room.

She was almost convinced. All she needed to do was think about it.

Think about it . . . and make the right decision.

WHEN THEY GOT BACK to the hotel, Wolenski was given access to the phone in Erika's suite, with Billy Two standing next to him.

"Don't make me nervous," Wolenski said to Billy as he started placing his calls.

He made three, trying to get his request into the right channels. His story was that he had a high roller in town who needed a woman on his arm—"a real stunner, you know, but a lady"—and was willing to pay big bucks for her. "Somebody like Julianne, you know?"

He listened then and his face fell, but then he said, "Well, send me the best you've got. Right. The Sheraton. Right. Suite sixteen-oh-five. Yeah. Whataya mean when? Right now!"

He hung up and looked at O'Toole.

"Well?" O'Toole said.

"The man said Julianne was unavailable."

"What's that mean?"

Wolenski shrugged. "It could mean anything from she left town to Kontiza . . . got rid of her."

"Killed her?"

"Or sold her."

"Sold her?" Erika repeated.

Wolenski looked at her. "He does that."

"So what's happening?" O'Toole asked.

"He's sending a girl up."

"What good will that do us?"

"When he sends one of his expensive ladies, he has her delivered. They wait for her, and then they drive her back to . . . wherever."

"So when she gets here her driver will wait downstairs?"

"Right."

"Okay," O'Toole said, "who wants to be the high roller?"

In the end it was decided that Jessup would be the high roller. Wolenski and George moved down to Jessup's room with Hatton and Erika. Claude Hayes stayed in the suite with Jessup, just in case.

O'Toole and Nanos staked out the lobby. Billy Two stayed outside, because even in the lobby of the big hotel he was too conspicuous waiting around. They were all armed with handguns, which they kept hidden. They would pick out the driver—or bodyguard—and isolate him. He would then take them to see Demetrius Kontiza, or he wouldn't be making any more deliveries.

Forty minutes later Billy Two saw a dark sedan pull up in front of the hotel. A man was driving, with a woman in the back seat. The man got out, opened the door for the woman and started to follow her into the hotel. He stopped briefly by the doorman and, in what looked like a prearranged move, handed the man something. A payoff? More than likely.

Billy Two crossed the street then and got in the car.

Inside the hotel O'Toole and Nanos spotted the woman with no difficulty. She was high-class merchandise, wearing a fur jacket and a short skirt. She had on high-heeled black sandals and black patterned stockings, and her blond hair was piled high on her head. Nanos looked across the lobby at O'Toole, raised his eyebrows and grinned.

A few steps behind the woman came the man. He wore a simple dark suit and followed her to the elevator. He waited there with her, but when she got on he stayed in the lobby.

O'Toole moved to a house phone and dialed Erika's suite.

"Yes?" Jessup answered.

"This looks like it," O'Toole said. "Any minute."

They kept the line open until Jessup said, "There's a knock on the door."

"Give Claude the phone."

Hayes came on and said, "Jessup's answering the door. Oh, Lordy, save me. Tall, blond and classy. Whoo!"

"That's her," O'Toole said. "Hold her."

"My pleasure." Hayes hung up.

O'Toole gave Nanos the high sign. The man was walking to the lobby doors, on his way out. The two SOBs fell in behind him.

The man went through the doors and walked to the car parked out front. Presumably he intended to wait there.

He went around to the driver's side as O'Toole and Nanos stepped out onto the street. They saw him open the driver's door and heard him say, "What the hell—" and no more.

O'Toole walked around the car while Nanos got into the back seat. Billy Two, sitting behind the wheel, had his Magnum jammed into the man's stomach.

O'Toole grabbed the man by the collar. "Get in the back," he said.

Billy Two turned and looked at Nanos, who had just settled into the back seat.

"The doorman," the big Osage said.

"I got him," Nanos said, and left the car. They wanted to make sure the doorman didn't make a phone call if he had seen what was taking place.

"What's going on?" the man demanded as O'Toole pushed him into the back seat and got in after him. Billy Two turned around and let his Magnum show over the back of the seat.

"We're going for a ride," O'Toole said. "My friend is going to drive, and you're going to give him directions."

"To where?" the man asked.

"To Kontiza."

At that moment Claude Hayes came out of the hotel and walked briskly to the car. He got in the front seat. The man in the back with O'Toole looked from Billy Two's native-American face to Claude Hayes's black one.

"Alex is taking the doorman upstairs," Claude told the others.

"We'll wait for him," O'Toole said. "That'll give our friend time to make up his mind what he wants to do."

"I don't know what you want—" the man started, but he stopped when Billy Two put away his gun and brought out his knife. He couldn't take his eyes off the knife after that.

"Play it smart, my friend," O'Toole advised. "Don't make me turn you over to my partners. They're a nasty pair, at best, and they haven't been at their best for some time now. They're in a real foul mood."

As if to show the man what foul moods they were in, both Billy Two and Claude Hayes scowled.

Sure, O'Toole thought, if I didn't know you guys, I'd be scared, too. It was all he could do to keep from laughing, but the threatening looks seemed to be working on the man.

A few moments later Nanos came out and got in the back seat. "I dropped the doorman off with Lee," he said.

"The woman is with Jessup," Hayes said.

"She's safe," Nanos said. "Jessup hasn't gone cannibal yet." Nanos noticed the mean facial expressions of Billy Two and Claude Hayes and asked, "What show are you two auditioning for?"

"What's your name, friend?" O'Toole asked the man next to him.

"J-James."

"You're kidding."

"No, I am not." The man frowned at O'Toole for a moment, then looked back at Billy Two and Claude.

"All right, then," O'Toole said to the man, "let's go."

"Go where?"

They all exchanged glances and said in unison, "Home, James!"

10

James directed Billy Two with a minimum of talk. Just a "Turn right here," or a "Bear left here," until the car was stopped outside an office building. The ride had taken ten minutes.

"I guess Kontiza likes to keep his business near the tourists," Nanos said, looking up at the building.

"All right, where is Kontiza's office?" O'Toole asked.

"The top floor," James said, as if the question was a foolish one.

"Silly me," O'Toole said. "You're going to take us up there."

"I'll be a dead man if I do," the man said nervously.

"You'll be a dead man if you don't," Nanos told him. "Make your choice. Now or later." From beneath his jacket Nanos produced one of the Mini-Uzis.

"When did you get that?" O'Toole asked.

"When I took the doorman upstairs," Nanos said. "I thought we might need a friend along."

"Good thinking," O'Toole said. He looked at James and asked, "What's your decision?"

"Later," James said.

"Then let's move."

They got out of the car and entered the lobby of the building, with the others surrounding James so he couldn't go anywhere.

"What kind of security does your boss have?"

"Not very much. No one would dare—" He stopped, realizing how silly that sounded in the present circumstances.

"Will you be stopped?" O'Toole asked.

"Of course not. I am very important," James said proudly.

"I'm sure all your boss's soldiers feel that way," Nanos said. "He's got a way about him, doesn't he?"

"Where to now?" O'Toole asked James.

"There is an elevator at the back of the lobby. It goes directly to the top floor."

"That's where we're going, then."

They walked through the lobby and Hayes whispered to the man, "Make the wrong sign to somebody and you're dead meat."

As they approached the elevator they saw two men leaning against the wall, one on each side. The men straightened and looked inquiringly at James. To his credit James simply nodded at them, and managed not to look too nervous doing it. The men returned his nod and returned to their relaxed stance.

"Very good," O'Toole said. "If it all goes this smoothly you may come out of this alive."

When they reached the elevator that would take them to the top floor they saw that they had a problem.

"It's too small," Hayes said, looking at the single door, which was closed now.

"How many of us will fit?" O'Toole asked the man.

"That depends on whether or not he is one of you," James said, looking at Billy Two.

"Let's say he's not."

"If we squeeze together, perhaps the four of us."

O'Toole frowned. "Billy, if he's right you'll have to come up alone, after us."

"That's okay."

"You won't know what's happening, so you'll have to be careful."

"I am always careful," Billy Two said. "Hawk Spirit will be with me."

"Good," O'Toole said. "There'll be room for him in the elevator, too."

"Here, take this." Nanos offered Billy Two the Mini-Uzi.

"Thanks, but I'll make do with this," Billy said, palming his Magnum.

"Suit yourself." Nanos slipped the Uzi back beneath his jacket.

"How do we get this elevator to operate?" O'Toole asked.

"I have to call it down." James indicated a phone next to the door.

"You do that, and watch what you say."

James picked up the receiver and put it to his ear. There was no dial or push buttons. Apparently the phone was activated as soon as the receiver was removed. Billy Two moved close to James so that he could listen, and also to remind the man that the wrong word would put him in imminent danger of ceasing to exist.

"Yes, it's James," the man said into the receiver. "Send the elevator down." Somebody said something and he said, "Never mind, just send it down!"

"What was that about?" O'Toole asked.

Billy Two answered. "Somebody on the other end wanted to know if the high roller had a short fuse."

"I'll have to tell Jessup about that," Nanos said.

A high-pitched whine came from behind the door, signaling that the elevator was on its way.

"What will we find upstairs?" O'Toole asked.

"Just a small hall outside of one door."

"How many men will be there?"

"Two."

"Armed?"

"Yes."

"How?"

"By preference. Handguns, mostly."

"The Uzi will impress them?"

"Oh, yes," James said, "it will impress them."

In a small, confined space a Mini-Uzi—with a twenty-round magazine and the capability of firing 950 9 mm parabellum rounds per minute—could hardly fail to be impressive.

The whine stopped and the door slid open. Nanos covered the interior with the Uzi, and when they were satisfied that it was empty O'Toole pushed James ahead of him and said, "You first."

James entered and stepped to the back. The elevator couldn't have been more than four feet square, and as the rest of them entered James began to get squashed against the back wall.

"Take deep breaths and hold 'em," Claude Hayes said, entering.

"Aren't you glad you use Dial?" Nanos sang.

Billy Two smiled at the sight of the four men squeezed inside the cage.

"Is this thing going to move?" Nanos wondered aloud.

"And if so, will we make it to the top?" Claude Hayes said.

"Hey, Billy," Nanos said as the door closed, "do you think you could lend us Hawk Spirit for a min—"

After the door closed Billy Two held the Magnum down against his right leg and looked all around at the elevator court and the lobby. People were going about their business, and nobody was paying him any more attention than a six and a half foot Indian in an Athens office building would normally attract.

The elevator glided upward smoothly but slowly.

"Alex?"

"Yeah, Claude?"

They were back-to-back and one couldn't breathe without the other feeling it.

"I sure hope you don't have your finger on the trigger of that Uzi."

"Just don't make any sudden moves and you won't find out."

"All right, you clowns, quiet," O'Toole said. "We're getting there. Alex, you're the first out, so be real careful."

"First out's the best place to be," Nanos said.

O'Toole and Hayes knew he was right. He'd have room to move if there was any shooting, while they'd be trapped in the interior of the elevator.

"You wouldn't want to switch—" O'Toole began.

"Too late, clown," Nanos said as the elevator jerked to a stop.

There were two guards in the small hall outside the elevator. When the door opened the first thing those men saw was a creature with four heads and a lot of arms and legs. It took a few moments for them to realize that there were actually four men in the elevator. By that time they were looking down the barrel of a Mini-Uzi, and they both knew what the weapon was capable of doing.

"Easy," one of them said to Nanos in Greek.

"Just put your backs against the wall, boys," Nanos replied, also in Greek. "Don't even twitch until my friends have pried themselves out of the elevator."

"What are you telling them?" Claude Hayes asked.

"The one about the farmer's daughter and the traveling computer salesman—"

"Let's get them patted down," O'Toole interrupted.

Nanos kept one eye on the two men and on James while O'Toole and Hayes relieved the guards of their weapons. One was carrying a .38, the other a .44 Magnum.

"Jesus," Nanos said to him in Greek, "if you fired that in here we'd all go deaf. You been watching Dirty Harry movies?"

"I love Dirty Harry movies," the man said seriously.

"That figures."

The only words O'Toole and Hayes understood were "Dirty Harry."

"Send the elevator back down for Billy," O'Toole said to James.

James leaned into the elevator and pressed a button. He barely got his head out before the door closed.

"What do you want?" one of the guards asked in English. He was the one who liked Dirty Harry. He directed the question to O'Toole, who he obviously felt was in charge.

"Just a talk with your boss," O'Toole replied. "How many men does he have inside with him?"

"None."

"Come on," O'Toole drawled, but the man insisted he was telling the truth.

"He is interviewing a new girl," the man went on to explain. "He never lets us watch his . . . interviews."

O'Toole understood what the man was saying. "Well, with any luck," he said to Hayes and Nanos, "we'll catch Kontiza with his pants down."

They listened to the high-pitched whine of the elevator as it stopped in the lobby, then began to ascend.

"Listen to that thing groan," Nanos said. "It wasn't built to carry six and a half feet of Osage Indian."

They waited tensely until the door opened and discharged Billy Two, who was holding his gun out in front of him.

"Any problems?" he asked.

"No," O'Toole said. "You?"

"A lot of stares, but no problems."

"Good." O'Toole turned to the Dirty Harry fan and said, "Open the door."

"I can't."

Nanos raised his Uzi and said, "Sure you can."

"No, you don't understand," the man said. "The door can only be opened from the inside."

"How do you get in?"

"We call on the intercom, but we are always told not to interrupt."

"Interrupt him," O'Toole said.

The man exchanged glances with James and the other guard.

"He will be very angry."

"We'll be very angry if you don't," Nanos said, nudging the man with the Uzi.

"He will not open the door," the man warned.

"Tell him it's an emergency."

"He will not even answer until he's finished."

"Do it!" Hayes said.

The guard shrugged and walked to the intercom next to the door. He pressed a button. They could hear the buzzer sound inside.

No answer.

"Hit it again," O'Toole said.

"I told you—"

"Look out," Nanos said, pushing the man aside. He put his thumb on the button and the buzzer sounded again, only he didn't remove his thumb. He leaned on the button and the buzzer seemed to become more insistent the longer it went on.

"What the hell?" An angry voice shouted from the box.

"Answer the man," Nanos said, stepping aside.

The Dirty Harry fan spoke into the intercom. "Mr. Kontiza, could you open the door?"

"What the hell is wrong with you morons?" Kontiza shouted in Greek.

O'Toole and Hayes looked at Nanos for a translation.

"He's pissed," Nanos explained.

"It's an emergency, Mr. Kontiza," the man said.

"What kind of emergency?"

The man looked at O'Toole, who in turn looked at Nanos, who pointed to James.

"James is back," the guard told his boss.

"So soon? What went wrong?"

Nanos shook his head and shrugged.

"I don't know, sir. He will only tell you."

"Son of a bitch!" Kontiza said, and they all understood that. "All right, I'm opening the door. This had better be good."

A different, harsher buzzer sounded, and Nanos moved to the door as the lock snapped open. He shoved the door open with his shoulder and went in with the Uzi ready.

Kontiza was standing behind a huge desk, stark naked. Undoubtedly he had recently experienced a lot of stimulation, but at the moment his excitement was flagging. At the sight of the Uzi it abated completely.

"What the fuck—" Kontiza said, and then he recognized Nanos.

Behind Nanos, Kontiza's men were being pushed into the room by O'Toole, Hayes and Billy Two, who entered behind them.

"Where's the girl?" Nanos asked.

"In the next room," Kontiza answered immediately. "She's no danger to you, unless she bites you."

"Alex," O'Toole said. Nanos moved toward the door that led to the next room and entered.

A woman was lying there on an unmade bed. She was nude and seemed to be writhing in expectation, and when she heard Nanos she moaned in English, "Oh, God, Jimmy, come and finish me, quick!"

"Sorry, honey, but Jimmy's dick is in a wringer," Nanos said. "Will I do?"

The woman sat up straight, drawing up her knees close to her chin, and stared at Nanos. She was in her early twenties, and had flaming red hair and a curvy body, with big breasts and long legs.

"Well, love, in a pinch I guess you would." She spoke with a pronounced Irish brogue, and there was no trace of fear in her voice.

She's a tough one, Nanos thought. "In a pinch?" he said aloud, his feelings hurt. "I've got an Irishman out here, how about him?"

"Trot him on in."

"Cheeky one, aren't you," he said.

"Alex, stop fooling around and bring her out," O'Toole barked from the other room.

The woman raised one eyebrow—Nanos had always wished he could do that—and asked, "Is that your Irishman?"

"It is."

"He doesn't sound like much fun."

"Come on outside, the fun's just starting."

"Can I put something on?"

"If you must," he said regretfully.

She rose from the bed, revealing herself to be tall, about five-eight. If she'd been shorter she might have been chunky. She picked up her dress from the floor and slipped it on. She didn't bother with underwear. "Shall we go?"

"After you, Colleen."

She gave Nanos a smile and said, "The name's Kerry O'Toole."

"You're kidding."

"Why would I?"

"Wait'll I introduce you."

She raised both eyebrows this time and sauntered past him into the other room, trailing the scent of expensive perfume and sex.

No one had moved in Kontiza's office, except that Kontiza's three men now stood noses to the wall.

"Gentlemen," Nanos said, "let me introduce Kerry O'Toole."

"You're kidding," Hayes said.

"What's wrong with my name?" she demanded, hands on hips.

"Nothing, love," Liam O'Toole told her. "It's perfect. Now just shut up for a while."

"Who does he think he—" she started to say, turning to face Nanos, but he showed her the barrel of the Uzi and she fell silent.

"Would you like to tell me what this is all about now?" Kontiza asked. For somebody who'd been caught with his pants off, he seemed pretty damn calm.

"Would you like to put something on?" O'Toole asked.

"Not unless you're embarrassed."

"Obviously you're not," O'Toole said. "Not embarrassed and not worried. How often do four armed men break into your office?"

"This is the first time," Kontiza said, "but the way I figure it, if you were here to kill me I would be dead. That means you want something from me. Is it something that couldn't be done through the proper channels?"

"It is," O'Toole said. "We're looking for one of your girls."

"What do *I* look like?" Kerry O'Toole asked. No one answered and she fell into a sullen silence.

"First guns, now women?" Kontiza asked.

"Not *women*," O'Toole said, "just one woman."

"Which one?"

"Her name is Julianne."

"Sorry."

"What does that mean?"

"I can't help you."

"Why not?"

"She's not with me anymore."

"What happened to her?"

"Nothing," Kontiza said. "As far as I know, she's safe and healthy."

"But *where* is she safe and healthy?" O'Toole asked. "That's what we want to know."

"How should I know?"

"Look—" O'Toole moved closer to Kontiza "—I think it's time we stopped playing games. I want to know where she is, and I want to know now."

Kontiza took a moment to light a cigarette from a box on his desk and then said, "Don't threaten me, friend. You're in my backyard, and you think you have the upper hand."

"And we don't?"

"No," Kontiza said. "See, I know you won't kill me, because you want something from me, so let's not be getting so tough."

O'Toole eyed Kontiza's smug face for a moment, then looked at Kerry O'Toole, who was no relation, but was as fine a looking Irish lass as he had ever seen.

"Is he any good?" he asked.

"He's very good," she said. "He knows how to please a woman, and he likes doing it—pleasing her, I mean."

"That's enough," O'Toole said. "Claude, Billy?"

"Yeah?" Claude said.

"Spread-eagle Mr. Kontiza on top of the desk."

"Wha—" Kontiza said, but before he could finish Hayes and Billy Two had lifted him off his feet. O'Toole swept everything off the desk and Kontiza was quickly spread-eagled there, Hayes holding his arms and Billy Two pinning his ankles.

O'Toole put his gun down and moved to Kontiza's feet. "I'll take the ankles," he told Billy. The big Osage released them and O'Toole leaned on them, pinning them securely.

"What the hell do you think you're doing?" Kontiza demanded. He was red-faced and struggling.

"*Now* it's harder to be such a cocksure fellow, isn't it?" O'Toole said.

"Let me up, damn it!"

"As soon as you answer my question."

"I'm not answering any questions in this position."

"Billy."

O'Toole didn't have to spell it out for the Osage. Billy took out his knife, and with his other hand grabbed hold of Kontiza's hair and yanked his head back. He lightly laid the sharp edge of his knife against the man's exposed neck, and leaned over to look into his eyes. "You've got a good head of hair there," Billy said in a conspiratorial tone.

"Heavens," Kerry O'Toole whispered.

"Hey, hey!" Kontiza said hoarsely. He had broken out into a sweat.

"One more time, Jimmy," O'Toole said, "and if I don't like the answer, remember that my friend wants a souvenir."

"Please, n-no!" Kontiza said in a near-whisper.

"Where's Julianne?"

"I don't have the bitch anymore," Kontiza shouted. "I sold her."

"Who to?"

"I don't know!"

"Billy—"

"Wait, Jesus, w-wait!"

"Who?"

"I don't know. H-he said his name was Joshua and that he wanted to buy her contract."

"You make your girls sign contracts?" O'Toole asked.

"Y-yes."

"Did you know that?" he asked Kerry O'Toole.

She shrugged. "It's not really worth the paper it's written on."

"All right," O'Toole said, "what does Joshua look like?"

"L-like a man who dunked his head in acid," Kontiza said. "His face is horribly scarred."

"So you sold Julianne to him."

"Y-yes. He offered a lot of money."

"Where was he taking her?"

"To an island."

"Now we're getting somewhere. What island?"

"Can't you make him let go?" Kontiza looked nervously at Billy Two.

"No," O'Toole replied.

"At least tell him to move the knife," Kontiza pleaded. "He's going to cut me whether he means to or not."

"Not yet, Jimmy. We aren't satisfied yet."

"Jesus Christ! All right. I had him tailed when he left."

"And?"

"He took a boat out, a charter."

"And?"

"And when the captain came back I asked him where he took him."

"And he said?"

"One of the small, undeveloped Cyclades."

"Is this captain still around?"

"Yes."

"So he could take us there."

"Y-yes, he could. Jesus, please!" Kontiza said.

"What's his name?"

"Stanapolous, Socrates Stanapolous. His boat is docked at Piraeus. Now, please. . ."

Billy Two looked at O'Toole, who nodded and removed his hands from Kontiza's ankles. Billy Two moved back and allowed the knife to dangle at his side, then put it back into its sheath. When Hayes let go of the wrists, Kontiza immediately sat up, desperate to feel more in control than when he had been flat on his back.

"What do you think?" Nanos asked O'Toole.

"I don't like it."

"What don't you like?" Nanos asked. "We just have to find this charter captain and have him run us out to the island."

"Why did Joshua use a charter, and then leave the captain alive to tell where he is? No, what I don't like is that we're getting an invitation that's been cloaked in subterfuge to make it *look* hard.''

"You mean..."

"I mean this scar-faced son of a bitch *wants* us to find him."

"And when we find him we find the colonel," Claude Hayes said.

"That's the bitch of it," O'Toole said. "He wants us to find him, and we're going to go ahead and do it anyway."

He turned to look at Kerry O'Toole and asked, "You still want to work for him?"

"Are you kidding? I don't even want to be here when he recovers. Do you mind if I leave with you?"

"Not at all," O'Toole said. "Claude, would you see the lady to the elevator?"

"Would it be all right if this gentlemen did that?" She indicated Alex Nanos.

O'Toole sighed as a slow smile spread over Nanos's handsome face. "Sure," Liam said. "Alex, do you mind?"

"Not at all."

Nanos passed the Mini-Uzi to Claude Hayes and took hold of Kerry O'Toole's elbow. They left the room together and entered the small elevator. O'Toole wondered if the thing moved slowly enough for those two to get better acquainted on the way down.

"Is there another way down from here?" O'Toole asked the other three men.

The Dirty Harry fan said, "There's a stairway in the back."

"Use it," O'Toole said to him, the other guard and James. All three men turned away from the wall and looked toward Kontiza.

"Trust me on this," O'Toole said. "When he gets back to his feet you don't want to be around."

The three men exchanged glances, then walked into the bedroom and out a rear door.

O'Toole walked over to where Kontiza was still lying on the desk and grabbed him by the hair. "Keep a low profile for a while, Jimmy," he said harshly. "If I see you, or if you get in my way, I'll have my friend come back, and then you will become a trophy—a cheap one, at that. Understand?"

Kontiza looked at O'Toole with tortured eyes, couldn't speak but managed to nod.

"Good," O'Toole said with a grin. "I'm glad we finally reached an understanding."

11

"Explain this to me again," Walker Jessup said.

"There's not much to explain," O'Toole said. "We've all been suckered."

They were back at the hotel, in Erika's suite, and O'Toole had just tried to explain his theory to Jessup and the others.

"You mean this man Joshua *doesn't* have Nile?" Erika asked hopefully.

"No, I think he has him, all right," O'Toole said, "but it looks to me like the purpose of taking the colonel was to get us all there trying to find him."

"So he actually wants us to find him," Jessup said.

"Yes."

"Why?"

O'Toole shrugged. "I guess we'll find that out when we get there," he said. "Won't we?"

IN THE AFTERNOON Joshua watched Dieter Muller work the men, just as he had in the morning. They were coming together as a team remarkably well, but as Muller had pointed out, they had all worked with one another at some time, so it was just a matter of becoming reacquainted.

By now, he thought, Kontiza will have given the SOBs Socrates's name—not willingly, but he will have given it. Buying Julianne from Kontiza had been one of Joshua's earliest moves in this chess game—the opening gambit—but now they were rapidly coming down to the endgame.

Joshua had always excelled at the endgame.

Julianne did not bring lunch to Barrabas, but she did bring dinner. This time when she removed the gag she also removed the blindfold, without being asked.

The signs were getting better and better, Barrabas thought.

They didn't talk much as she fed him dinner—lamb again—but afterward she didn't replace the gag, and didn't make a move to leave.

"Have you made a decision, Julianne?" he asked gently.

"Yes."

"What is it?"

"I have to get away," she said, sitting with her hands in her lap, "but I'm frightened."

"Cut me loose."

"I can't," she said. "Not yet."

"When?"

"When I'm ready," she said. "When I've built up the courage."

"Will you be able to get me a weapon?"

"I...I don't know."

"What about the man, Julianne," he asked. "The man who's holding us both here. Who is he?"

"I don't know. He calls himself Joshua."

"No other name?"

"N-no." Clearly, talking about this man made her extremely nervous. Barrabas decided to put off any more talk about him until next time.

"Do this for me, then," he said. "Loosen my bonds. I've been tied for a long time and my hands are numb." He hoped that his hands weren't permanently impaired by this time. "I need to get the blood circulating again."

"I don't know...."

"Just loosen them—" He stopped himself when he realized he was close to snapping at her. He didn't want to push her over the edge, away from him. "Just loosen them," he said again more gently. "That's all."

She thought a moment, then said, "All right."

She got on her knees behind him, but he didn't feel her touch his bonds.

"There," she said.

"You've done it?"

"Yes."

He didn't feel a thing. His hands were totally numb!

"And my legs?"

He felt her balk.

"Just loosen them," he said.

She obeyed. As she loosened the ropes around his ankles he felt pinpricks of blood rushing through his feet. Apparently they had not been tied as tightly as his hands. He still felt nothing there. The painful pricking of blood starting to circulate again would be welcome. He hoped it would come soon.

Julianne replaced the gag and blindfold, also looser than before, and then gathered up the plate and utensils.

"I mean what I told you last time," she said to him, her mouth close to his ear. "If you get me out of here alive I'll be yours forever."

If he hadn't been gagged he would have told her that wouldn't be necessary. He wanted to get out of there even more than she did, and if she helped him he would just naturally take her along.

He listened as she went out the door and up the steps. The only sounds he ever heard were her comings and goings, and occasionally voices from above, though not loud enough to hear what was said. Apparently the cellar was deep enough that sounds from outside did not penetrate the walls or ceiling.

He wondered what the hell was going on outside.

"COME ON, MULLER," Sam Bowen prodded. "You can tell us who this guy is."

"He'll tell you when the time comes," Dieter Muller said.

"You're taking this second-in-command business very seriously, *mon ami*," Marcel DuLac said.

"I take every aspect of our business seriously, DuLac," Muller said. "You should try it some time."

"I do. I'm still alive, aren't I?" DuLac said with a laugh.

"That can change very quickly," Muller returned.

They were all seated around a fire, eating their dinner.

"Why are we out here while he stays in there?" Angus McFadden asked.

"Because that's the way he wants it," Muller said.

"And the woman," DuLac said, his eyes widening. "Have any of you seen the woman?"

"Only a glimpse," Bowen said. "Enough to know she's a real beauty."

"Mon ami," DuLac said, "beauty does not describe her."

"Anybody get a closer look?" Bowen asked.

The others shook their heads, except for Muller, who did not reply.

"Muller," Handy Hyde said, "what about you? Have you seen her up close?"

"I've seen her," Muller said.

"Jesus, is she a real looker?" Bowen asked. "How old is she? What kind of tits—"

"All I know is that she's his woman," Muller said. "Beyond that I don't think about her."

"What are you, made of stone, man?" Bowen asked.

"Could we cut out the bullshit about the woman?" Muller said. "According to the man our opposition should be arriving sometime tomorrow. We have to be ready."

"Hell, we are ready," Handy Hyde said. "We're ready for any team."

"Come on, Muller," Bowen said. "Who are we going up against?"

"All I know is that they're a crack team, and they've been together a long time."

"But we've got the home-field advantage," Bowen reminded them all. "We know every inch of this rock and they don't."

"That will certainly be in our favor," Muller said.

"Do you know who they are, Muller?" Hyde asked.

"I only know what he's told me."

"You say 'he' like we're talking about the Almighty," Sam Bowen said.

"Not quite," Muller said.

No, not the Almighty, he thought. More like the devil himself.

IT WAS DIFFICULT for Julianne to make love to Joshua that night—more difficult than ever before.

He thought she loved oral sex, but the truth was she would rather suck his cock than look at his face. He was actually a very skillful lover, and she had achieved some of the most powerful orgasms of her life with him, but her skin crawled whenever he kissed her, and she became frenzied in her lovemaking in order not to cringe—or run from him.

She had not been happy working for Demetrius Kontiza, but after he sold her to Joshua she had realized it hadn't been such a bad life. At least when she was working she had been free to move around on her own. Since Joshua had brought her to his island she had virtually been confined to the house and the area around it. Now, with the arrival of the other men, her confinement had narrowed to the house itself. He didn't even like her to go to the window, although she had done so several times. She had seen the men drilling then, and she knew they had seen her.

Her only time of peace was when she was in the cellar feeding Barrabas. He was the only man on the island she felt she could trust.

Tomorrow, she thought, tomorrow she would free him from the cellar.

Barrabas, the man Joshua feared, the man who would save her life.

Tomorrow.

THAT NIGHT Nanos and Billy Two took Wolenski and his man George to their room and tied them to chairs. It was merely a safety precaution. They'd be released in the morning. George was grateful not to have to spend any more time in a closet. The hotel doorman, who might or might not have been working for Kontiza, had already been released, and had run for his life.

Walker Jessup stayed in his room alone. The call girl had been sent home with a generous tip. He knew that he'd be staying behind tomorrow, with Erika. He was no match for the SOBs in the field, and if he tried to tag along he'd only slow them down.

Hayes and O'Toole went to their room. Hayes went to bed, while O'Toole sat up until very late in a comfortable chair.

"Liam, you'd better get some sleep," Hayes said finally from his bed. "We have a big day tomorrow."

"I know, Claude, I know."

"What's bothering you?"

O'Toole turned and looked at Hayes. "I'm just wondering if we've done everything we could."

"Bullshit." Hayes sat up in bed. "You're wondering if *you've* done all you could do."

O'Toole looked away. "Maybe."

"You've done what's had to be done, Liam," Hayes said. "Nobody's said any different."

"I know."

"We're all going to follow you tomorrow, Liam," Hayes said. "That's the way it has to be. They may be waiting for us, but we've got to go out there."

"What do you think about Kontiza?" O'Toole asked.

"You mean is he going to rat us out? I don't think so. Besides, if the man behind all this wants us to find him, it doesn't really matter."

"We should have gone tonight."

"On a boat among those islands? At night? Hell, even an experienced seaman wouldn't do that. Alex knows that, and so do you."

"I know, I know."

"Get to bed, Liam. We can't have you falling asleep on us tomorrow."

"Yeah, okay." O'Toole turned off the lamp, sat there a few more moments, then slid into bed. He laced his hands behind his head and stared at the ceiling.

Alex Nanos, too, had gone to bed. He watched Billy Two, who was silently communing with Hawk Spirit. The look on the big Osage's face was one of total peace.

Sometimes Nanos wished he believed in Hawk Spirit. He could use that kind of peace himself.

In her suite Erika Dykstra lay awake in the bed she had shared with Nile Barrabas before this nightmare had begun. She wished there was something more she could do tomorrow than just sit and wait. Of course, she understood that if she accompanied the others—which they would probably never permit, anyway—they would be distracted by her presence and the need to keep her from being hurt.

In the end, she knew that the best thing she could do was stay behind and out of trouble. If anyone could find Barrabas and bring him back safely, it was the people he'd been working with so long, and so well.

Of course, that didn't help her to sleep any better.

Lee Hatton slept on the sofa in Erika's room. She could have gone back to her own room, but she thought Barrabas wouldn't have wanted Erika to be left alone.

All through this crisis, Hatton had been suffering uncomfortable qualms of guilt. She knew such feelings were silly, but the fact was, it was her name that had been used to lure Barrabas from the hotel. He had gone out to help her, because he was a man who would never say no to a friend. Somehow she felt she owed him for that.

For that, and a whole lot more.

BARRABAS WAS ELATED at the thought that this might be his last night in this underground prison.

He felt sure that Julianne would come down tomorrow to bring him breakfast, and would release him then. If things really went well, she'd have a weapon with her, and some information about what he'd be up against when he got outside.

Outside, in the sun. He knew his eyes were going to have to get used to the sun, but at least his legs felt okay, and although his hands were still tingling, they weren't numb anymore.

As he worked his hands, just to get the blood going and keep it going, he realized that Julianne hadn't just loosened the ropes on his wrists, she had loosened them *a lot*!

Anxiously he began working his hands and wrists even harder. Maybe, just maybe he'd be able to get loose by morning.

Upstairs in the house, while Julianne slept, Joshua slid out of bed. Naked, he stepped outside. He liked the way the sea breeze wafted over him, stirring his hair.

Actually, more than half the hair wasn't even his, it was grafted on, but the surgeons had said it would be just like his own. They were wrong. It was only his own hair that stirred in the breeze, the other just sat there, unmoving.

He spread his legs so he could feel the soothing wind on his genitals, still damp from Julianne. At least the hair there was all his, and it also stirred with the breeze.

He wouldn't be able to sleep tonight, he knew that. Already the slow passage of time was driving him crazy.

Talking to someone might help. But to whom? Julianne? No, he'd bought her for several reasons, but talking wasn't one of them.

Dieter Muller? No, the man wouldn't understand, and neither would any of the others.

Who was left?

Only one person.

And he would understand.

When Barrabas heard the footsteps on the stairs he stopped manipulating his fingers, although one hand was almost free. Why was she coming back now? To free him?

Then, as he listened intently to the footsteps, he knew they weren't Julianne's. They were heavier, the strides longer.

Someone else was coming down.

Who?

And why?

To kill him?

He knew he couldn't free his hands in the next few seconds, so he didn't bother trying. He just sat quietly and waited to see what was going to happen.

12

At the hotel in Athens, they all woke early and assembled in Erika's suite. As each entered, he was surprised to see the others at that hour. Erika said, "I'll order breakfast for everyone."

"Billy and I might as well bring Wolenski and George up here, too," Nanos said. "We'll give them breakfast and send them on their way."

"I guess we're all too worked up to sleep," O'Toole said as Alex and the Osage went out.

"Who's worked up?" Jessup said. "I got up because I was hungry."

"Sure," O'Toole said.

Hayes, O'Toole and Hatton began to check their weapons, which—with the exception of handguns—had been left in the suite overnight. All the guns appropriated at Wolenski's house were in excellent condition. When Nanos and Billy Two returned with Wolenski and George in tow, the weapons were laid out on the coffee table.

"Jesus," Wolenski said, "it looks like you're going to war."

"We are," Hayes said.

"With Joshua?"

O'Toole looked at him, and then nodded.

"Good. Cut off his balls for me."

"Why?"

"He set me up."

"You figured that out, too?" O'Toole said. "He set us all up."

"And you're going out to that island, anyway?" Wolenski asked, in disbelief. "Knowing that?"

"He's got a friend of ours out there," Hatton said, "and we want him back."

"He must be a pretty special friend."

They all exchanged glances, but let Erika be the spokesperson. "He is," she said softly.

There was a knock on the door. "That must be room service," Jessup said. "Cover the guns."

They pulled a sheet off the sofa where Hatton had slept and spread it over the coffee table.

The food was wheeled in and everyone discovered they were hungry. Wolenski and George's wrists were untied.

"What are you going to do with me and George?" Wolenski asked as he dug into the contents of a loaded plate.

"After breakfast you can leave," O'Toole said. "Or, if you like, you can leave now."

"I'd just as soon eat first."

George nodded in agreement, his mouth full of eggs.

Conversation was sporadic as they all applied their attention to the food. No one mentioned that if things went badly, this would be their last meal.

No one had to.

BARRABAS WAS RECOVERING from his shock.

When the door opened and the man walked in, he

had sat there waiting, half expecting to be killed. Several minutes went by, during which he knew he was being watched. Gagged as he was, he couldn't ask who was there. He sat quietly and willed himself to be patient.

It was amazing how you could almost feel a watcher's eyes move over your body.

Finally the man had spoken. "Hello, Colonel."

The voice was instantly recognizable. Barrabas could hardly believe his ears, for he had thought the speaker to have died at least three years before.

"Yes, it's me," the man had said. "Wait, I'll take off your gag, and your blindfold."

Barrabas felt the hands roughly pull the blindfold down and the gag out of his mouth. He squeezed his eyes shut a moment, then opened them slowly. The man had brought a storm lantern with him, and its glow lit the room adequately, without blinding Barrabas.

He looked at the man, and in spite of the disfigured face, he recognized him immediately.

"Thomas Gilkenny."

"The same, though they call me Joshua these days," Gilkenny had answered. He was naked to the waist, having hastily donned trousers and boots before coming to the cellar. "Take a good look, Nile," he'd said, "look at the man who's going to pay you back, after all this time."

Barrabas looked at him, looked past the scarred face to the eyes. Looking into his eyes he'd immediately known one thing for sure—the man was mad!

They had talked through what was left of the night.

Gilkenny had told Barrabas the story of his life over the past three years. The months and months of intense pain while trying to recover from his injuries; the planning that had been done during those months, and the steps taken to bring those plans to fruition—to bring himself, and Barrabas, and the SOBs to this day, when it would all end.

"Why my people, Gilkenny?" Barrabas asked now.

"Why not?" Gilkenny asked. "Didn't *my* people die?"

"That was a war... of sorts," Barrabas said lamely.

"So is this a war," Gilkenny said, his voice rough. "This is my war, Gilkenny's war against Barrabas. I've got six men up there, Nile, six of the best fighting men in the world, and this is their home base. Your people will be here soon to rescue you, and they'll be wiped out. And when it's over, and they're all dead, I'll come down and get you and show them to you—just before I kill you."

"You're crazy, Gilkenny," Barrabas said. "Your mind's been warped by some imagined injustice I've done you."

"Imagined?" Gilkenny asked, staggering back a couple of steps as if he'd been struck. "Imagined injustice? Is that what you call it?"

"You had your chance—"

"Shut up!" Gilkenny shouted.

"I had a job—"

"Shut up!" He moved forward swiftly and slapped Barrabas in the face. The blow caught him on the ear and his head began to ring. At that moment he found himself hoping that Gilkenny wouldn't check his hands and feet.

Gilkenny turned away from him and walked to the door, leaving the gag and blindfold off in his anger. At the door he turned.

"Sit here, Barrabas, and think about what's waiting for your people when they get here. They're walking into an ambush, just like me and my people did three years ago—only they won't be as lucky as I was. I'm still alive, and they're going to be dead."

"Look at yourself, Gilkenny," Barrabas said. "Is that what you call being alive?"

Gilkenny's face flushed a deep red, and Barrabas thought that if the man had had a gun at that moment he would have killed him. Instead, Gilkenny stormed out of the room, slamming the door behind him. Barrabas listened to the key in the lock and then to Gilkenny's footsteps as the man angrily ran up the steps.

He waited a few moments, to see if Gilkenny had gone upstairs for a gun. When there was no sound of him returning, he again began to work on his bonds with renewed vigor.

Now that he knew what was going to happen, he had to get free. He had to warn O'Toole and the others that they were walking into a trap, but he couldn't do that if he was tied up!

PIRAEUS, THE PORT where Socrates Stanapolous had his fishing boat docked, was only fifteen minutes from downtown Athens. O'Toole and the other SOBs piled into Wolenski's Citroën, which he told them they could leave in Piraeus without worry of returning it.

"You fellas have enough to worry about. I'll have the car picked up later."

Wolenski also wished them luck. He appeared to view them no longer as enemies but as friends. It was obvious the change was the result of his wish for the worst for the man Joshua.

In the car on the way to Piraeus Alex Nanos said, "I wonder if this fella Joshua will turn out to be someone we know, or if he's just someone from the colonel's past."

"We'll find out soon enough," O'Toole said. "Let's hope that after today he's a part of all our pasts."

If he wasn't, they would probably all be dead.

When they reached the port the SOBs parked the Citroën and piled out.

"Make sure it's locked," Claude Hayes said. They all looked at him. He shrugged. "We don't know if they steal cars around here."

Billy Two leaned into the car and locked all the doors.

There was no way they could hide the fact that they were heavily armed. They all had Berettas that had been taken from Wolenski's men at his house, except for Billy Two, who was carrying the Magnum. O'Toole, Hayes and Hatton had Mini-Uzis, while Nanos and Billy Two carried AK-47s that had also been taken from Wolenski's men.

They moved onto the dock and spotted the boat, an old fishing scow with the name *Achilles* flaking off the back. As they approached it a barrel-chested, robust-looking man in his sixties stepped onto the dock and appeared to be expecting them.

"Jesus," Nanos said, "*everyone* knows we're coming."

"Captain Stanapolous?" O'Toole inquired.

"Yes?"

"We'd like you to take us to an island."

"I understand."

"You've been notified?"

"Yes." Stanapolous was eyeing them nervously. He had been informed by radio message from Joshua that some men would be seeking out him and his boat today, and that he was to transport them to the island. Joshua was paying him a lot of money, but Stanapolous was worried that these men might harm him, or worse, kill him when they got to the island.

O'Toole realized the seaman was worried that he was going to be harmed. "We only want you to take us there, Captain. We mean you no harm."

"I take no sides in this," the man said. "I do what I do for money."

"We understand that," O'Toole replied. "We usually do what we do for money. It is a good reason."

"Not a noble reason, but a good one," Stanapolous agreed. "Shall we go now?"

"Yes, please," O'Toole said, "the sooner the better."

The veteran sailor heaved a sigh, still not completely relieved of anxiety. He fervently hoped that this morning had not been the last time he would ever see his new twenty-five-year-old wife.

GILKENNY LOOKED DOWN at the island's only dock, with Dieter Muller standing next to him.

"We could kill them right on the dock," Muller suggested, "as they get off the boat. We could even booby-trap the dock so that it blows up."

"I want them taken fairly." Gilkenny looked at Muller. "That's why I brought you and the others here.

I want the Soldiers of Barrabas removed by a better team."

"Well, we're a better team," Muller said. "I know a couple of the SOBs, and I certainly know Barrabas, but without Barrabas the SOBs are not the same team."

"I know that," Gilkenny said, "and I've set up this whole happening to prove that to Barrabas."

"You must really hate him."

Gilkenny touched his ruined face. "Hate is much too mild a word for what I feel for Nile Barrabas." He pulled his hand away and said, "Get your men ready. They should be here any minute."

"Is that it?" O'Toole asked, pointing to land on the horizon. He'd asked the question at least a dozen times during the trip, revealing how tense he was.

This time the old captain nodded his head. "Yes, that's it."

"Where will you drop us?"

"On the dock."

"Is there only one dock?"

"Yes."

O'Toole wiped some sea spray from his face and thought about that one dock. He turned and looked at the other SOBs, and wondered how bad a situation—or trap—he was leading them into.

"I have an idea," he said to Stanapolous, and the old captain listened intently.

"Are your men in position?"

"They are."

Gilkenny and Muller watched the dock together and scanned the horizon for signs of a boat.

"Wait," Gilkenny said. "I hear it."

Muller listened and said, "I hear it too, but I don't see it."

Gilkenny listened intently, then slapped Muller on the back and laughed.

"What?"

"They're not landing on the dock," Gilkenny said. "But the old man has foxed them anyway. He's bringing them close enough for us to hear the boat. He's alerted us. Get your men, get your men! It's time!"

After all these months, these years, it was time.

STANAPOLOUS WAS SORRY he had had to lie to this man, O'Toole, about there being no other locations on the island where they could have disembarked. But this was the closest to the dock, and the sound of the boat would alert Joshua. If O'Toole found out about his deception, he'd kill him, but if Stanapolous had dropped them anywhere else, he knew Joshua would kill him.

Joshua was evil. It was not his scarred face that made Stanapolous believe that; it was the man's eyes. O'Toole did not have eyes like that, and in the end that had been the reason for his decision.

O'Toole knew, of course, that the captain was lying. He had agreed to drop them someplace other than the dock, but was probably dropping them close enough for the sound of the boat to be heard. Still, by not landing on the dock they at least had a chance to get off the boat; otherwise they could have been blasted right off the dock.

Stanapolous stopped his engines and the boat floated about twenty feet offshore.

"You'll have to walk in from here. It's not deep enough for me to get closer, and it's shallow enough for you and your people to walk."

"All right, Captain." O'Toole looked into the eyes of the old man and said, "You did what you had to do."

The old man looked away. There seemed to be words he wanted to say, but they were stuck in his throat.

"Let's go," O'Toole said to the others. "Move it. We don't have that much time."

The SOBs gathered onshore, soaked to the knees, but with their weapons as dry as they could be after the ride they'd just taken. They were *soaked* to the knees because they had had to wade ashore, but they were damp all over from the sea spray they'd had to travel through.

"Look at this." Nanos scuffed at the ground underfoot. "It's mostly solid rock." That was all he could see, except for the small patch of sand they were standing in.

"The dock is that way—" O'Toole pointed to his right "—so we'll go this way," and he pointed to the left. "We'll try and circle around and come in behind the dock."

"We need to find some high ground so we can see the whole island," Billy Two said. "I can—"

"I think we should stay together for now, Billy," O'Toole said.

"I can move just ahead of the rest of you," Billy Two suggested. "There might be some booby traps."

"All right," O'Toole agreed, "but don't leave our sight."

Billy gave O'Toole a thumbs-up sign and headed off.

"All right, let's move, but spread out," O'Toole ordered. "I don't want one burst of fire taking us all out. We're the only chance the colonel has."

If he's even here, Hatton thought. Then she thrust that thought away. He had to be here, or they were risking their lives for nothing.

"THEY'LL TRY to circle around," Dieter Muller told his men. "We'll work our way back and find some cover, and wait for them."

"And ambush them?" Handy Hyde said.

"Can you think of a better way?"

"I thought you said this Joshua wanted them taken on even terms."

"Even terms?" Muller said, snorting. "That's why he's sending six of us against five of them, right? That's why he's lured them out here, right? He's stacked the deck against them every step of the way."

"Then we can take them without ambushing them—" Hyde started.

"That sense of fair play you have went out of this business a long time ago, pop," Sam Bowen said to Hyde.

"It was never there, my friend," Marcel DuLac said. "Our friend Handy is too idealistic to make a good mercenary."

"I'm still alive," Handy Hyde said.

DuLac smiled and said, "A careful mercenary, yes, but not a good one."

Hyde was about to reply when Muller said, "That's enough. While you argue, they're getting closer."

"Who are these guys, anyway?" Elmore Kirk asked. "We've got to know what we're up against now."

"All right," Muller said. "They're called the Soldiers of Barrabas."

"The SOBs?" Handy Hyde asked in astonishment. "Nile Barrabas's group?"

"Never heard of them," Sam Bowen said.

"They don't advertise," Hyde said. "But believe me, they're as rough a bunch as there is."

"Not as rough as we are," Bowen said cockily.

Muller and Hyde were the only two men who had heard of the SOBs, but Kirk and DuLac knew who Barrabas was.

"Barrabas is not an easy man to outmaneuver, *mon ami*," DuLac said to Dieter Muller.

"We don't have to worry about that," Muller said.

"What do you mean?"

"Joshua's already done that," Muller explained. "He's got Barrabas tied up in his cellar."

"And he hasn't killed him?" Hyde asked. "Barrabas is a bad one to play games with. Who is this guy Joshua, anyway? Don't we get to know that?"

Muller thought a moment, then decided to go ahead and tell them. "Have you ever heard of a man named Gilkenny? Thomas Gilkenny?"

"Sure," Handy Hyde said. "Helluva fighting man, but a little too vicious for my taste. He died somewhere in Africa a few years ago."

"No, he didn't," Muller said.

Hyde stared at Muller for a few moments. "Joshua is Thomas Gilkenny?"

"Yes."

"But Gilkenny burned to death."

"Most of his face is gone, but Joshua is Gilkenny," Muller said. "I know the man."

"So do I." A look of distaste crossed Hyde's face. "Did you collect up front?"

"What's that mean?" Sam Bowen asked. "This guy Joshua—I mean Gilkenny—is he gonna stiff us?"

"He will not stiff us," Muller said.

"You're sure of that?" Hyde asked.

"I'm sure."

"I've heard of Gilkenny," Angus McFadden said. "Where's he getting the money for this operation?"

"I didn't ask," Muller said, "but I'm satisfied that he has it."

"I don't know Gilkenny," DuLac said, "but I know I want my money, and to get it we have to kill these Soldiers of Barrabas. And we will not do it standing here, *mes amis*."

"Marcel is right," Muller said. "We've got to get moving. Anybody who wants out, speak up now."

They all shuffled their feet and exchanged glances, but no one spoke up.

"All right, then," Muller said, "let's move."

JULIANNE KNEW that Gilkenny would be out of the house for a long time now. He was going to wait for the men he called the Soldiers of Barrabas to arrive. He had chosen the highest point on the island—a rocky plateau—to watch the upcoming contest.

This was her chance to release Barrabas so they could escape together during the confusion. She had even managed to find him a gun.

She grabbed the gun now, and a knife, too, and started down the stairs.

In the cellar, Barrabas paced, his hands and feet free now. He had tried the heavy basement door, but there was no way he could open it.

He wished Gilkenny had not stayed with him so long. He would have liked to pace and stretch a little longer to work the kinks out of his arms and legs. Everything considered, though, he felt pretty good.

He heard the upper door open and then the footsteps on the stairs. He flattened himself against the wall next to the door, just in case it wasn't Julianne.

But he was sure it was.

Julianne gasped when she entered the cellar and saw Barrabas.

"You're free!" she exclaimed.

"Well, I'm not tied up anymore," he said, pulling her inside, "but I'm not exactly free." He closed the door behind her.

"I came to untie you," she said, still confused by finding him untied.

"I worked that out myself. He put his hand on her back, establishing contact. This was the first time he'd been standing with her in the room, and he saw that she was nearly as tall as he was.

"Tell me what's happening," he said.

"Joshua—"

"Gilkenny."

"What?"

"That's his real name, Thomas Gilkenny. You didn't know that?"

"No, I only know him as Joshua."

"All right, go on."

"He's expecting some men today, so he's out, watching the dock, I think, with Muller."

"Muller? Dieter Muller?"

"I think so, yes. Do you know him?"

"I know him, yes. Do you know who else is here?"

"Four or five other men. I don't know their names."

"Well, if Gilkenny has Muller here, he probably has some other men of equal ability, and by now they know the terrain."

"These other men who are coming, do you know them?"

"I know them, yes."

"Now that you are free, can we go? Can we escape now?"

"Julianne—" he took hold of her arm "—the men who are coming are walking into a trap. I have to try and help them."

"But you are supposed to help me escape," she said urgently. "You promised!"

"And I will keep my promise," he said, "but I can't desert my friends. Hell, they're coming here to rescue me! Now we can all rescue one another."

"Or get killed," she said, showing signs of petulance.

"Julianne, did you bring me a weapon?"

"Yes." She brought her hand around from behind her back. "I found a gun."

He stared at it, then took it from her. "A gun," he said.

"Yes. Is it a good gun?"

"It's a Very pistol."

"Is that good?"

The Very pistol fires flares, which are used at sea to call for help.

He snapped it open and checked it. Well, he thought, at least it's loaded.

"Sure," he said, "it's fine."

13

"Man, you've got to be a mountain goat!" Claude Hayes said as he slipped on a rock, cutting his hand again. He let out a muted curse and paused to suck on the small but painful cut.

"Billy Two isn't having any trouble," Nanos said from behind. He had put his hands on Hayes's hips to steady him. He had already slipped once, too, and had a nick on his palm to show for it. These rocks were sharp.

"That's because that big Indian *is* part mountain goat," Hayes said.

The terrain gradually sloped higher and higher as they were climbing. As a consequence their progress had slowed. O'Toole saw Billy Two coming back toward them. He stopped their progress abruptly to wait for him.

"There's a high point that looks to be in the center of the island," Billy Two said.

"Can we get to it?"

"Not easily, but there's one other thing."

"What's that?"

"There's already someone up there."

"A spotter?" O'Toole asked.

"Or a spectator."

"Is he armed?"

"Not that I could see." Billy Two had the Starlite binocs around his neck.

"What about a radio?"

"Didn't see any, but that doesn't mean it's not there."

"So maybe he's a spectator," O'Toole said. "Maybe that's Joshua, and he's got himself a ringside seat."

"That's my bet," Billy Two said.

"Well," O'Toole said, "we'll try and put on a good show for him. What else did you see?"

"Nothing. The terrain is very craggy, and there could be a man behind every rock, for all we know."

"What does Hawk Spirit tell you?"

For an instant Billy Two looked surprised that O'Toole would even ask such a question, but then he said, "Sometimes Hawk Spirit leaves me to my own devices."

"Which are considerable," O'Toole said.

Billy Two didn't comment.

O'Toole took a moment to consider the situation, then said, "All right, maybe it is time to split up. Since we may be walking into a trap, there's no reason for all of us to do so. Billy, we'll continue on as we're going and then we'll cut south and head for the dock area. Why don't you cut across the terrain and see what you can find? You're probably the only one who can move around on this damned rock without cutting yourself to ribbons." O'Toole had a cut on his knee for his trouble. "There's got to be a house or a shack around here somewhere, where they're keeping the colonel."

"And if I find the house?"

"See if you can get to it and get to the colonel," O'Toole said. "Maybe you can free him while we keep

Joshua's attention diverted—and the attention of whatever or whoever he throws at us."

"And if I find Joshua?"

O'Toole looked in the big Osage Indian's eyes. He wanted it spelled out. "Get rid of him."

FROM HIS VANTAGE POINT on the island's highest peak Gilkenny could see Muller and his men secreting themselves in the craggy terrain of the island. Gilkenny had chosen this island for two reasons. One was the rugged, rocky terrain, and the other was this peak he was standing on. It was important to him to have a good vantage point for watching his team defeat and kill the SOBs.

He had a gun with him—Barrabas's P-38, which was tucked into the back of his belt. He did not have a radio. He had considered bringing a radio with him for directing his men, but had decided against it. The time it would take him to relay his instructions to Muller, and then for Muller to relay them to his men, would put them at a disadvantage. He had decided to rely on Dieter Muller's leadership qualities, which were considerable, and the reason he had chosen Muller in the first place.

The SOBs had not yet come into view, but from his position he had seen Socrates Stanapolous's boat leave the area. It wouldn't be long before the SOBs would stumble their way into view.

Gilkenny licked his lips in anticipation.

BARRABAS LED THE WAY up the steps, the Very pistol held ready. Behind him, holding his hand extremely tight, trailed Julianne.

They entered the small house and he was surprised. The cellar below was larger than the structure on top.

Julianne said, "Joshua once told me that smugglers used this place many years ago."

"It makes sense," Barrabas said. "They had plenty of room downstairs to store booty, and a tiny house up top that wouldn't attract undue attention."

He moved to the window and looked out cautiously. He could see the dock, but no boat.

"Julianne, does Joshua have a boat?"

"No."

He turned to look at her in surprise. "How did you expect us to escape?"

She stared at him hopelessly and shrugged.

"How does Joshua get off the island?"

"He doesn't. Since we've been here he's hardly been off the island. He has a radio, and anything we've needed he calls for."

Barrabas frowned. He would have preferred to have a boat at his disposal. Now he was going to have to get to the radio and call...who? Oh, well, he thought, maybe the SOBs had brought a boat with them.

"Where would Gilkenny be now?" he asked.

"There's a high point in the center of the island," she said. "You have to go outside to the back of the house to see it. I think he was going to watch from there."

"All right," he said. "You're going to have to stay here, Julianne, while I go outside."

"But you'll get killed!" she cried. "Then who will take me away from here?"

"I won't get killed," Barrabas assured her. "Just stay here so I don't have to worry about you."

She crossed her arms beneath her breasts. The action reminded him that she was still wearing a bikini.

"Do you have any other clothes?"

"Yes, but Joshua wants me to dress this way."

"Well, change your clothes," he said, trying to distract her. "When we leave here, I want you dressed. I have enough problems without having to keep a bunch of horny men away from you."

"Horny?" She frowned.

"Never mind," he said. "Just stay put."

Barrabas left the shack cautiously, staying close to the wall as he walked around to the back. From there he could see the highest peak on the island. There was a man up there.

Gilkenny.

Gilkenny was not facing his way, but was looking elsewhere on the island. Barrabas imagined that Gilkenny was watching a battle in the making, between his private army and the SOBs.

Grasping the Very gun tight in his hand, Barrabas decided that the most direct action he could take was to reach Gilkenny and try to put a stop to the battle before it started. Whoever the men were whom Gilkenny had hired—and whom Dieter Muller was leading—they were only doing what they were paid to do. If Barrabas could get to Gilkenny and force him to call the battle off, he could save the lives of everyone involved, and not just the SOBs.

Without his realizing it, Barrabas's thoughts right now would have proved to an impartial adjudicator what the difference had always been between Thomas Gilkenny and himself.

O'TOOLE AND THE OTHER SOBs—minus Billy Two—crested a rise. From there they could see the man on the high peak, but no one else.

"There are so many nooks and crannies on this island, they could be anywhere," O'Toole said.

"What choice have we got?" Nanos asked.

"We can circle back around the way we came," O'Toole replied.

"Retrace our steps? That'd be a waste of the time we spent getting here."

"Yeah, but if they heard the boat coming, then they have to expect us to come this way, to circle around and come at them from behind."

"If you're reading them right," Claude Hayes said.

"There's only one way *to* read them," O'Toole stated.

"How's that?" Hatton asked.

"We have to assume they're the very best Joshua could find. That means they'll probably do what we would do."

"I know there's a compliment in there somewhere," Alex Nanos said.

"All right, let's do this," O'Toole suggested. "I'll take Lee and go back the way we came, to come at them from the dock. Alex, you and Claude stay here and keep an eye out. Maybe they'll get impatient and come out of hiding. If that happens, you can pick them off."

"And if they're not even here?" Hayes asked. "If you and Lee walk into their waiting arms?"

"Then you'll be the ones to come up on them from behind and bail us out," Hatton said.

"Excuse me," Nanos said, "aren't you the guy who said we shouldn't split up?"

O'Toole looked at Nanos. "I changed my mind."

Nanos shrugged. "Just asking." Then he looked at Hayes. "You game?"

"I'm always game."

Nanos said to O'Toole, "Let's go for it."

DIETER MULLER was tucked into one of the island's nooks or crannies with Handy Hyde. About twenty feet from them in every direction were Sam Bowen, Elmore Kirk, Marcel DuLac and Angus McFadden. From Muller's position, he could see Thomas Gilkenny, who was standing like a statue, watching.

"Look at him," Hyde said, "up there, out of harm's way, watching us down here like he was watching a television program."

"He's paying for that right," Muller said.

"Maybe," Hyde said, "but I don't like it. It's... chickenshit."

Muller looked at him and said, "Chickenshit?"

"Cowardly," Hyde translated. "He used to be a pretty good fighting man, but now he's lost it."

"After what he's been through, I'm not surprised," Muller said.

"I'd rather die," Hyde said, "than lose it and become what he is—a civilian."

Muller didn't answer. He didn't relish the thought of eventually becoming a civilian, either. Almost any career soldier or merc would rather die in battle than return to civilian life. But maybe, Muller thought, maybe

Thomas Gilkenny *had* died in battle, and what was left rose from the ashes and became Joshua.

"What's keeping them?" Hyde asked, changing the subject and jarring Muller from his reverie.

"They don't know the terrain," Muller said. "They're traveling slowly."

After a pause, Hyde said, "Or they're not coming."

"What do you mean?"

"Just what I said," Hyde said. "What if they went back the way they came? What if they're heading straight for the dock?"

Muller thought a moment. "The boat did land fairly close to us. If they thought we heard it, they'd expect us to cover the back door, right?"

"Right."

"Very well, Handy," Muller said, "take Bowen and DuLac and cover the dock."

"Right."

Hyde rose and started to leave his hiding place. At that moment there was a burst of fire. Lead struck the rocks near him, kicking up rock splinters. He leaped back in beside Muller. "They're here."

"DID YOU GET HIM?" Hayes asked.

"No," Nanos said, "but I scared the shit out of him."

"We've got to keep them pinned down until O'Toole and Hatton can work their way around."

Nanos, cradling his AK-47, said, "Next time we'll fire together. It's got to sound like there's more than two of us."

Hayes was holding his Mini-Uzi in one hand. He removed his Beretta 93-R machine pistol from the holster and set it for semiautomatic 3-round bursts. "Let's kick up some dust," he said.

They stood up then and began to fire, Nanos holding his AK-47 in both hands, Hayes holding the Beretta in one and the Uzi in the other. Together they kicked up dust and enough sharp slivers of rock to blind a small army.

Handy Hyde covered his head and face as rock splinters flew everywhere. When the firing stopped he pulled two such fragments from the back of his right hand.

"Handy, you've got to get out of here and take Bowen and DuLac to the dock," Muller said. He had pulled a sharp piece of rock from his cheek, under his left eye, and left a smear of blood there.

"Why, for Chrissake?"

"Because they're not all there," Muller said.

"How do you know that?"

"There's too much firing going on, with no targets in clear sight," Muller explained. "They're trying to make us think that there are more men firing than there really are. The others are trying to circle back to the dock."

"How do you propose I get out of here?" Hyde asked.

"We'll cover you. Just pass the word to the others."

Hyde gave the situation some thought and decided Muller was right. Even if Muller wasn't right, he was in charge of this operation and had to be obeyed, but it was easier to follow orders when you agreed with your leader.

"All right, give me some cover," Hyde said.

"I'll fire now for cover. Tell the others that the next time I fire they should fire, as well. That's when you'll move."

"Right."

Muller stood and began to fire his Beretta AR70. All his men had been outfitted with AR70s and also carried the Beretta 93-R pistol. The AR70's were fitted with thirty-round magazines. They could also fire 40 mm rifle grenades, which Muller had decided to keep in reserve as a potential surprise.

Gilkenny had told Muller that the only guns the SOBs would have been able to get were Mini-Uzis, but to Muller's educated ear it seemed someone on the other side had been using an AK-47.

He fired a long burst so that Hyde could crawl over to Bowen and then DuLac, and pass the word to the rest of the men.

Muller ducked back down and fed a new thirty-round box into the AR70, waited sixty seconds, then stood and fired again. Behind him he could hear McFadden and Kirk also firing. He didn't risk a look, but he knew that Hyde, Bowen and DuLac would be scrambling away, heading for the dock area.

After the firing had stopped, Nanos asked, "What do you think?"

"I think they've got some pretty good firepower," Hayes said, brushing stone chips from his hair.

"I'll take a look," Nanos said.

As he started to look up the firing began again, this time even heavier. Before sliding down, though, he saw that two or three of the men were scrambling away.

"Great!" he shouted. "Some of them have gone back to the dock."

Hayes opened his mouth to reply, then decided to wait until the gunfire stopped.

In the ensuing silence he said, "O'Toole and Hatton will have to handle them. We're separated into two different fights now. Let's hope we can deal with both."

"Well, we still have our ace in the hole," Nanos said, "if Billy can get to the colonel."

"Let's give these birds something to think about," Hayes said.

Nanos nodded, and the two of them stood and squeezed their triggers.

This is a game, Nanos couldn't help thinking. He would have preferred some good old jungle fighting anytime.

GILKENNY WATCHED with pleasure as his men outmaneuvered the SOBs. He couldn't see Barrabas's men but he could imagine what had happened, and was delighted his men had not fallen for it. Soon, another battle would take place by the dock, and he also had a clear view of that one.

Maybe Barrabas would even be able to hear the firing in the cellar, and then curiosity and frustration would really make him sweat.

BARRABAS WAS FEELING a little sweaty at that point, but otherwise calm and controlled. Far from being frustrated, he found his mind was operating quickly and efficiently to plan a course of action. He heard the firing and knew that his SOBs had engaged Muller and his men. The battle had all of Gilkenny's attention, and Barrabas was able to work his way behind the peak

Gilkenny was sitting on. All he had to do was find a path to climb and he'd be behind the man.

BILLY TWO HAD ALMOST reached the house when he heard the firing. He stopped for a moment, his thoughts with his colleagues, then shook his head and continued. There was no point in worrying about them. They had their jobs, and he had his.

He could see the observer from where he was. The man's attention was directed toward the firing, enabling Billy Two to move to the house and flatten himself against the side. Now the observer wouldn't see him even if he did look this way.

Billy Two moved around to the front of the house and stopped right next to the door. He listened for a moment, then stood in front of the door and slammed his heel into it, just above the doorknob.

As he leaped into the room the naked woman turned with a gasp and looked at him. He'd interrupted her dressing. There were a couple of wisps of clothing on the floor—both parts of a bikini—and some other clothes on the bed. She was holding a garment, but it was too small for her to hide behind. He saw round, solid breasts with brown nipples, and bushy black pubic hair.

"Don't move," he said, and his eyes darted around the interior.

"He's gone," she said, finding her voice.

"What?"

"Barrabas," she said, "he's gone."

He frowned. "Where?"

"He's gone after Joshua," she said, "the man he called Gilkenny."

Gilkenny! Billy Two knew that name well. Now everything fell into place.

He studied the woman—her face, that is, for at that moment he had no interest in her body—and decided that she was telling the truth. "How did he get away?"

"I was going to let him, go, but he freed himself of his bonds. I let him out of the cellar."

"Is he armed?"

"He has some kind of a gun."

"What kind?"

"I don't know. I—I had the feeling he was disappointed when I gave it to him."

"Describe it."

She did so, also describing how Barrabas had broken it open to see if it was loaded. Billy Two recognized that it was a flare gun, not exactly Barrabas's first choice of weapon.

"M-may I get dressed?" she asked.

"Yes, go ahead."

As she dressed he searched the dwelling and found no weapons. When he turned back to her she was wearing jeans and a shirt that was tied beneath her breasts.

"I have to go after him," Billy said. "You stay inside."

"That's what he told me."

"Then do it," he said. "It would be very dangerous to go outside."

She nodded, her eyes wide. She had been as startled by his appearance as he had been by hers. She had never seen a man so large.

"I'll stay inside."

Billy Two nodded, then backed toward the door and stepped out.

Barrabas had gone after Gilkenny, who was obviously the observer, and he was virtually unarmed.

Billy moved around to the opposite side of the building from where he had approached. Immediately the wall next to him was struck by a hail of bullets and he hit the ground as the firing continued. The wall was stitched directly above him, where he had been standing a moment ago. He lifted his head and saw three men firing at him. In moments they'd find his range and riddle him with bullets, and he had nowhere to go.

Well, he thought, lifting his AK-47, he might as well take somebody with him.

He didn't realize reinforcements were approaching.

O'Toole and Hatton had had to walk a stone ledge almost the whole way to the dock, once they'd left Hayes and Nanos. Beyond the dock they saw a clearing of dirt with a small house standing in the center of it. A small shack, possibly a radio shack, was perched beyond the main building.

"Keep down," O'Toole told Hatton. They had no way of knowing who was in the house.

"The door!" Hatton whispered.

O'Toole saw the door to the house open and then a huge man stepped out. It was Billy Two.

They watched as Billy glided around to the side of the house, and then they saw three men move into the clearing.

"Come on," O'Toole said.

They were running toward the house when the men opened fire and they saw Billy Two go down. Not knowing if he was hit or not they both raised their Mini-Uzis and began to fire.

Billy Two heard the shooting coming from behind him and knew that help had arrived either just in time, or just too late, depending on how the opposition reacted. If they ignored the new arrivals and continued to fire at him, he was finished. If, however, they were distracted, then he had a chance.

He lay there and watched the three men. One of them stopped firing and pointed, then the other two stopped. They all turned their guns away from Billy—possibly thinking he had been hit—and opened up on the new arrivals.

Billy rose to his knees then, gripping his AK-47 in both hands, and squeezed the trigger. One man spun as he was hit. The other two fell to their knees, then began to back away.

Billy ran toward them. Hawk Spirit had saved him by bringing help. His feet barely touched the ground because he could feel Hawk Spirit within him.

O'Toole and Hatton saw Billy Two rise as the three enemies turned their attention away from him toward them.

They separated, putting a lot of room between them, so they couldn't both be taken out by the same burst of fire. As they did so they saw Billy fire and one of the other men fall.

Billy then started charging the two remaining men, and he was closer to them than Hatton and O'Toole were.

Faster, O'Toole told his legs. He marveled at the speed with which Billy Two was moving. It wasn't natural.

Billy Two continued to fire, and then as the AK-47 ran out of ammo the big Osage took out his Magnum and began to shoot with that.

By this time O'Toole had pulled away from Hatton, who could not keep up. She simply dropped to her knees and, replacing the empty ammo box with a fresh one, kept firing, covering him. O'Toole reloaded on the run. Approaching from a slightly different direction than Billy Two, the two SOBs had the remaining pair of enemies in something of a cross fire.

HANDY HYDE LOOKED DOWN at the fallen Sam Bowen. He'd thought the man by the house had been hit, but obviously he'd been wrong. Now Bowen was dead and they were outnumbered three to two.

The big man they had initially fired at was running toward them at amazing speed, firing his AK-47, while the other two—Jesus, was one of them a woman?—were also approaching, armed with Mini-Uzis.

"Back," he shouted at Marcel DuLac, but DuLac's blood lust was up. Hyde had heard that rumored about DuLac, that reason fled from him when he had his finger on the trigger.

"Jesus," Hyde said. As long as DuLac remained, he'd have to stay with him.

He turned to face the oncoming rush of the huge man, who had discarded his AK-47 and was now holding a handgun. He fired at him at what he considered point-blank range, and somehow managed to miss.

I'm getting old, Hyde lamented. In the next moment a slug from Billy Two's Magnum struck him in the forehead, and he would get no older.

DuLac was unaware of what was happening around him. Instead, as had happened so many times before, he was filled with electricity, as if it were coming from the trigger of his gun. He bit his lip as he fired, feeling his eyes blaze hot. He loved this, loved it even more than he loved women—and *was* that a woman firing at him now? His two greatest loves in one place—women and death.

What more could a man—and a Frenchman, at that—ask for?

As he turned to train his gun on O'Toole it suddenly stopped chattering. He tried to reload quickly, but a burst from O'Toole's Mini-Uzi caught him in the chest, and his first love, death, took him to her bosom.

O'TOOLE AND BILLY TWO checked the bodies as Hatton ran toward them.

"Are you all right?" she asked both of them.

"Fine," O'Toole said, and Billy Two nodded.

She addressed Billy Two. "You're not."

"What?"

O'Toole looked at the big Osage and saw that he was bleeding, apparently from the neck.

"Billy, you're hit."

"Where?" Billy Two was so filled with Hawk Spirit that he felt no pain.

"Your neck," Dr. Leona Hatton said, moving closer to take a look. She examined the wound. "A bullet cut a furrow here and kept going. It's not bad."

"Worry about it later," Billy Two said. "There's a woman inside who says the colonel has gone after Gilkenny."

"Gilkenny?" O'Toole echoed. "Thomas Gilkenny? He's dead."

"According to what the colonel told her," Billy Two said, "that's him up there."

At that moment, as they were looking up at him, the observer turned and looked at them. They couldn't see his face, but suddenly O'Toole felt something pass through the air between them, something malevolent, evil.

"That's him," he agreed, without raising the Starlite binocs to his eyes.

Gilkenny looked toward the house and saw three people standing.

No, he thought, this can't be right. He knew they were SOBs. He could see the size of the big one, the damned Indian, and he recognized the shape of the woman.

Goddammit, they'd killed his men.

What had gone wrong?

The SOBs down by the shack heard gunfire.

"Hayes and Nanos need help," O'Toole said. "Billy, go after the colonel. When you reach him, give him this." He handed Billy the Colonel's P-38. "When he meets Gilkenny he's going to want it."

"I'll catch him," Billy Two said.

As Billy Two took off after Barrabas, O'Toole searched one of the dead men.

"Jesus," he said when he found the 40 mm rifle grenades. He discarded his Mini-Uzi and picked up the man's AR70. Hatton moved to one of the other dead men and did the same.

O'Toole turned to Hatton then and said, "Let's go bail their sorry asses out."

14

"We can't just sit here," Nanos said. "We fire, they fire, and none of us has a clear target. It's stupid."

"What do you suggest?"

"Let's rush 'em."

"What else do you suggest?"

"We've got to do something."

Suddenly an explosion occurred very near them and a shower of stone and dirt came down on them.

"Christ," Hayes said, "let's get out of here."

Muller, who agreed with Nanos's assessment of the situation, decided to bring out the surprise. He loaded the rifle grenades into his weapon and fired in the general direction of the SOBs. The grenade bullet hit and immediately detonated, sending a shower of rock debris through the air.

That'll keep their heads down, he thought.

He stood up and shouted, "Let's go!"

He fired another grenade bullet for good measure and he, Kirk and McFadden charged behind it.

Gilkenny watched as Muller led two of his men—McFadden, by the looks of him, and one other—in a charge. If they could wipe out their opponents, then there was still a chance of victory.

He reached behind him to grasp Barrabas's P-38 and pulled it out of his waistband.

Meanwhile, Hayes and Nanos were heading back the way they had come, the way O'Toole and Hatton had gone not long ago. They had no defense against rifle grenades, and nothing to meet them with, so the best thing they could do was fall back and regroup with the others.

When Muller and his men reached the point of the two explosions, they saw that the SOBs had retreated.

"Which way?" Kirk asked.

"Back the way they came," Muller said. "They'll head for the dock. McFadden, you go back that way and join the others. Kirk and I will trail them."

"Right," the big Scot said.

They separated. Muller licked his lips. They had the SOBs on the run, which put him and his men at a definite advantage.

He wondered how Hyde and the other men were doing.

He wondered how Gilkenny was enjoying the show.

IT WAS VIRTUALLY IMPOSSIBLE to track someone over hard dirt and stone—normally, that is. Billy Two could feel Hawk Spirit nestled in his chest, and his eyes caught scuff marks on the stone that looked fairly recent.

He followed the faint trail until he was behind the peak that Gilkenny was using for his observation of the proceedings.

Billy Two couldn't see Barrabas between his position and the base of the peak, so he started to move his eyes upward. Suddenly he caught a flash of movement, and then he saw him. The pleasure that he felt at actually seeing Barrabas, knowing that he was alive, caused his face to light up with a radiant smile for a moment. He started to run then, closing the distance between himself and the base of the peak. Barrabas wasn't scaling the wall of the peak, which meant there had to be some sort of trail to the top, maybe an old smuggler's trail. He was sure that after days of being captive in the cellar of that house, Barrabas couldn't possibly be operating at full efficiency. Maybe he could catch up to the colonel before he reached the top, before he went into a face-off with Gilkenny, unarmed.

Barrabas had not been surprised to find the path. It was almost like a stairway cut into the face of the peak, a further indication that this island had been used in the past by smugglers.

It was a relief to him not to have to scale the wall. He wasn't sure he'd have had the strength for that. Even now he was feeling fatigued, and he wasn't more than halfway up.

He stopped to rest a moment.

O'TOOLE AND HATTON were traveling in the direction they thought would take them back to where they had left Nanos and Hayes. They looked up at Gilkenny on his peak and knew that if he had had a rifle up there he could have picked them off. From what O'Toole remembered of Gilkenny, the man was a sharpshooter.

He wondered why Gilkenny didn't have a gun. Why was he leaving the fighting to others?

O'Toole's thoughts were interrupted when they came face-to-face with a big man, almost as big as Billy Two. The man stopped short when he saw them and they all three stared at one another.

The big man spoke first.

"Well, lass," he said to Hatton, "which of you will it be to try me?"

"McFadden," O'Toole said.

The big man switched his gaze from Hatton to O'Toole. "I know you?" he asked.

"Maybe not. That doesn't matter. I've heard of you. Why don't you put your weapon down and walk away, McFadden? Three of your colleagues are already dead."

"You got them, huh? Well, three of your partners are dead, too."

"Really?" O'Toole said.

"I counted the bodies myself."

That was interesting. Apparently McFadden and his crew knew that there were five SOBs. But what he didn't know was that O'Toole and Hatton had split from Nanos and Hayes *after* Billy Two had already gone his own way. The man didn't know there were only two SOBs that he and his colleagues could have killed.

So he had to be lying, and Nanos and Hayes were still alive.

"I don't think so," O'Toole said.

"You calling me a liar?" McFadden demanded.

"It didn't sound like that to me," Hatton said.

"What did it sound like to you, lass?" McFadden asked.

"It sounded like he was questioning your ability to count."

McFadden frowned, thinking that the woman was calling him stupid. He wasn't that far off.

"What do we do now, McFadden? Slap leather and draw?"

They didn't need to slap leather. They all had weapons in their hands. If they all started firing at once, there was a good possibility that they'd all die.

"Looks like a standoff, huh?" McFadden said.

"Not really," O'Toole said. He reached out and touched Hatton's shoulder and she moved away from him, as he started moving away from her.

"There are two of us," O'Toole said as the distance between himself and Hatton widened.

McFadden's eyes moved from one to the other, but he'd hesitated too long. They were too far apart for him to take them both out with one burst.

"I'll take one of you with me," he said.

"There's no need for any of us to die," Hatton said.

"Wrong, lass," McFadden said, "there is."

"Pride?" she asked.

"Right," McFadden said. Smiling, he turned his gun toward her.

O'Toole fired seconds before Hatton did, and McFadden's finger tightened on the trigger of his AR70 as the slugs from O'Toole's rifle struck him in the chest.

O'Toole had almost forgotten that he'd loaded the confiscated AR70 with grenade bullets. When they struck McFadden they just about blew the man in half. His rifle stopped in midchatter.

O'Toole turned to look at Hatton, who was on her knees.

"Lee!" He rushed to her and saw that she'd been hit in the left arm. "Lee, how is it?"

"It hurts," she said, looking at him. "How do you think it is?" Her face was white, belying the light tone of her voice, and he knew she was in pain.

"Let me do what I can and we'll move on," he said.

"Leave it," she said. "I'm the doctor, remember? I'll take care of it, you go on."

"All right, I'll go on, but which way?"

"What . . . do you mean?" she asked, wincing.

"Well, they sent King Kong there back this way for some reason. Maybe Nanos and Hayes are on the run, and he was trying to head them off."

"At the dock?"

O'Toole nodded. "It all goes back to the dock, where we should have landed in the first place," he said, "and that's where I'm heading."

"Good luck," she said. "I'll be along shortly."

He gave her right shoulder a squeeze, then left her.

GILKENNY WATCHED McFadden blown to bits and swore. Not only were his men falling, but the SOBs had picked up some of the AR70's.

Well, if they defeated all his men they'd have to come up to the peak for him, and he was ready for them.

He reached over and settled his hand on the detonator he had brought up with him.

He was ready.

NANOS AND HAYES reached the beach where they had first landed.

"Let's keep going," Nanos said. "There's no decent cover here."

"We could go out into the water."

"Sure," Nanos said. "Is your gun waterproof?"

"Well, let's do this." Hayes put his gun down and peeled off his jacket. Nanos watched as Hayes threw the jacket down just at the edge of the water.

"You think that'll work?" he asked. He also put his gun down and removed his jacket. He tossed his into the water, so that it floated there, obvious evidence that they had discarded their jackets and gone into the water to hide.

"We'll see." Hayes picked up his rifle. "Let's go."

Nanos retrieved his weapon and followed the black man. They rounded a bend and waited. There wasn't much cover if the ruse didn't work and the men following them came around the bend. They'd all be in the open, and the ensuing firefight could wipe them all out. When you were dealing with machine pistols and rifles, even a dying hand could fire a fatal burst.

Moments later Dieter Muller and Elmore Kirk reached the stretch of beach where the SOBs had arrived on the island. Plenty of footprints in the wet sand demonstrated that.

"Look!" Kirk pointed at two discarded jackets, one floating in the water, the other on the beach at the edge of the water. "They've gone into the water," he said.

Squinting his eyes, Dieter Muller said, "Maybe."

"Look, there are footprints leading to the water's edge."

"There are footprints leading away, as well," Muller pointed out.

His hands tightened on his weapon. He didn't like the feel of the situation. "Come," he said.

"Where?"

"Back the way we came."

"We're assuming they're dead?" Kirk asked. "Drowned?"

"No, we're assuming that they're dangerous, and cunning. Come, we'll rejoin the others. When we're at full force, we will hunt them. If, indeed, they have drowned in the water, we lose nothing.''

Kirk shrugged. Muller was the boss, and he followed him back the way they had just come.

Nanos thought he heard the voices fade. He risked a look.

''They're leaving, and there's only two of them.''

''The hunted,'' Claude Hayes said, ''become the hunters.''

Nanos nodded. They both stepped from their cover.

Nanos and Hayes stalked the two men for about a hundred yards. Then, when they rounded a bend, the men were suddenly gone from sight.

''Uh-oh,'' Hayes said.

''Yeah.''

Hayes looked up at the stone wall on their right.

''You think they went up there?'' Nanos asked.

''I don't know. They went somewhere. They couldn't have gotten so far ahead of us that we wouldn't see them. There's not another bend for a couple of hundred yards.''

''If they're up there,'' Nanos said, ''we're sitting ducks.''

''Then I suggest we spread our wings,'' Hayes said.

They turned to retrace their steps when suddenly the quiet was shattered by a burst of fire. Lead chewed up the rocky earth immediately in front of them. They reversed direction. Another blast followed the first, this one kicking up the ground behind them.

''Shit,'' Nanos said, flattening himself against the wall. ''They're up there, all right!''

PARTWAY UP THE SLOPE, Barrabas felt his breath coming in dry rasps, tearing at his lungs and chest. He was annoyed by his weakness. But he was almost there, and the desire to end this thing between him and Gilkenny kept him going, albeit at a much slower pace.

From his vantage point at the top of the peak, Gilkenny could see only two of the SOBs. Where were the rest? he asked himself. Where were the rest of his men?

The heat of the day was beginning to tell on the combatants, even on the almost motionless Gilkenny. Although he was only watching, the flat stone peak he was sitting on had become nearly as hot as a frying pan. He could feel the heat through the soles of his boots, on the back of his neck, on his disfigured face. But Gilkenny had endured heat much, much worse than this, and had survived what few men could even have endured.

The fingers of his left hand curled around the barrel of Barrabas's P-38, and the fingers of his right rested lightly on the plunger of the detonator. The wires from the detonator extended to the edge of the peak, where he had dug holes and installed plastic explosives. At the flick of his hand they would carry an electrical charge to the plastic, igniting it and blowing the top of the peak clear off.

If the heat didn't do it first.

The time was nearing, he could feel it. If Barrabas's men had won the battle, then Barrabas himself would soon join him here on his peak.

And the final scene would be played out.

At the center of the island, Billy Two had found the crude stairway that some force had cut into the wall of the peak, and was ascending quickly. Above he could hear someone else moving, more slowly than he. He was sure it was Colonel Barrabas.

"Colonel!"

Barrabas paused, thinking he had heard someone call him, then continued on.

"Barrabas!" Billy Two's voice called.

Barrabas stopped and look behind him. Billy Two's huge frame came into view, and the big Osage smiled.

"Billy!"

Billy Two approached his superior and suppressed the urge to hug him. "You might need this," he said.

Barrabas looked at the P-38 Billy Two held in his hand, then accepted it. "Thanks."

"It's good to see you, sir."

"You too," Barrabas said. "Now do me a favor."

"What's that?"

"Stay right here." Barrabas tucked the P-38 into his belt and handed Billy the Very gun. "I'll be right back."

Against his better judgment Billy Two said, "Yes, sir."

"I CAN'T GET a clear shot, dammit," Elmore Kirk complained. "The fucking nigger and his friend are flat against the wall of rock."

"Keep firing," Muller told him. "You'll kick up dust and slivers of stone that may not be fatal, but they'll be painful, maybe harass them into making a foolish move."

"I hear you." He pointed his AR70 straight down and let loose with an entire clip.

As Kirk reloaded, Muller moved to the edge and said, "My turn."

O'TOOLE REACHED THE DOCK and saw that no one was there. Had he made the wrong choice? If he had, it wouldn't be the first time.

He turned and sent a random look over the part of the island he could see. Somewhere Hatton was bleeding, Billy Two was searching for Barrabas, Barrabas was looking for Gilkenny, Nanos and Hayes were either stalking or being stalked, and from his eagle's nest Gilkenny was watching the performance he had worked so hard to arrange.

O'Toole decided to go back to find Lee Hatton.

She wasn't far away.

"I was looking for you," she said as they neared each other. Her face was drawn and pale, but she seemed to be moving pretty well. He decided not to ask her if she was all right. It was probably the last question she wanted to hear.

"We might as well head back this way," O'Toole said, indicating the way she had come. "There's nobody at the dock."

"Where are they, then?" she asked.

"I don't know." He was worried about Hayes and Nanos. "Wandering around out there somewhere, I guess, playing cat and mouse with what's left of Gilkenny's men."

"Well, let's find them, then," Hatton said.

At that moment both O'Toole and Hatton looked up at Gilkenny, on his peak.

"By now he knows some of his men are dead, and yet he just stays up there, watching. What's he planning?" O'Toole wondered.

"I guess we'll have to leave that part of it to Billy and the colonel," Hatton said.

"That's right."

Just then they heard firing and tried to pinpoint the direction.

"Does sound bounce off stone?" she asked.

He frowned and said, "Beats me. It sounds like it's coming from over there."

He led the way and she followed as best she could. Her arm wound was painful. She was trying her best to ignore it when all she really wanted to do was sit down and rock herself. She tried not to think about infection....

BARRABAS COULD SEE the top now, and suddenly he could hear a man's voice. He couldn't make out all the words, but the tone told him plenty about the speaker's state of mind.

As he drew nearer he heard Gilkenny cursing. Whether he was cursing out his own people or the SOBs, Barrabas couldn't tell.

Cautiously, as he reached the top, Barrabas peered up at Gilkenny. The man's back was to Barrabas as he crouched on his haunches, watching the action below. It would have been easy to put a slug in him that way. Instead Barrabas climbed a few more steps to the summit and stood there. They were standing on a plateau about twelve feet in diameter.

Barrabas knew Gilkenny had heard him. He waited for the embittered man to turn.

"It's about time you got here," Gilkenny said, still offering Barrabas the temptation to shoot him in the back.

"You expected me."

"Of course I did," Gilkenny said. "You don't think I expected you to stay in that cellar while your people were being killed, did you?"

"Actually, it's your people who are being killed."

"You're right, of course," Gilkenny said. Still he did not turn around.

Barrabas tried to figure what Gilkenny was thinking and feeling. He surely was not as calm as he appeared. After all, his obsession had been to show Barrabas the bodies of his slain friends and soldiers. He would not be able to do that now. Such frustration would be enough to unsettle a stable personality, and Gilkenny had gone over the edge to insanity long before today's contest. If all he'd wanted to do was kill Barrabas he'd had plenty of opportunity to do that.

Of course, the man might figure that with his other plans in ruins, he'd settle now for the death of Barrabas alone.

"Have you got a gun?" Gilkenny asked.

"I have."

"So have I. What shall we do, turn and fire?"

Barrabas didn't answer.

"Or you could just put one in my back... But you wouldn't do that, would you?"

Again Barrabas didn't answer.

"I'm going to move now," Gilkenny said, "but I'm only moving to the side. I want to show you something."

Still crouched, Gilkenny moved several feet to his right. For the first time, Barrabas saw the plunger.

"Dynamite?" he asked.

"Plastic," Gilkenny said. "Old and unstable, too. Just the heat up here might be enough to set it off."

Barrabas could feel the heat striking him on the face, beating down on his neck and arms, intensified even more as it reflected off the flat stone floor where they stood.

"Gilkenny, let's get down from here, talk things over down there out of the sun."

"Afraid to die, Barrabas?"

"If I was I'd have gotten out of this business a long time ago."

"I'm not afraid to die." Gilkenny turned and added, "I died a long time ago."

Barrabas couldn't help wincing as the man turned and his ruined face came into view. It looked even worse now, reddened from the hours of exposure to the sun. In some places the skin looked as if it were seething with bubbles that were about to burst.

"I've got your gun, Barrabas," he said, showing the merc leader his P-38, "but I see you've found another. One of your people let you loose, huh?"

"No. Julianne did."

"The whore," Gilkenny said. "I chose her well, didn't I? She's incredible in bed. Is that what she offered you if you'd help her?"

"We agreed to help each other."

"Yes, just as I planned."

"Things aren't going the way you planned, Gilkenny," Barrabas pointed out. "Your people are getting killed."

"They're not all dead yet," Gilkenny said. "Some of your people might yet die."

"They might, but they've been prepared for that for a long time."

"Sure," Gilkenny said skeptically. "I thought I was prepared to die, too. When my face and body were on fire I thought I wanted to die...until I was staring death in the face. *Then* I knew I wasn't ready."

"And you're ready now?"

"If I can take you with me."

"That's bullshit, Thomas. If that's all you wanted you could have killed me and then yourself long ago."

"Yes, you're right. I wanted to make you suffer first, watching your people die." Gilkenny looked behind him as they heard the sound of shooting in the distance. Again Barrabas saw a chance to kill Gilkenny, but stayed his hand.

"Perhaps that's them, dying now," Gilkenny said.

"Or your people."

"No," Gilkenny said, looking at Barrabas. "They're not my people, they're just men I hired. I don't care if they live or die. You're different. You don't care if you live or die, but you do care about your people."

"Yes, I do."

"I don't care about anyone anymore," Gilkenny said flatly, "not even myself. Now I truly am ready to die. Death is better than living like this." His fingers moved lightly over the puckered livid flesh of his disfigurement.

More than the man's face had been ruined by the fire in Africa, Barrabas realized. The man's mind had been damaged, as well. Even if plastic surgery could have repaired his face, was there any medical science that could restore his twisted reason? Once, Gilkenny had been a brilliant tactician—a little headstrong, but brilliant.

"Gilkenny, let's go down. Your face can be fixed—"

"I don't want it *fixed*!" Gilkenny said. "I want it back the way it used to be. I want the pain to go away. I want the memories to go away. Can anyone do that for me?"

Barrabas didn't answer.

"No," Gilkenny said, answering his own question, "no one can do that for me, only I can." He looked at the plunger and said, "I can do that . . . now."

"WE'LL HAVE TO MAKE a run for it in opposite directions," Nanos proposed. "Maybe one of us will get away."

"Yeah," Hayes agreed, "Maybe one of us."

They looked at each other. Then Nanos said, "Good luck."

"Luck, Alex," Hayes said gruffly.

They gripped their weapons tightly and readied themselves to run.

THERE HAD BEEN SILENCE on the hilltop for a minute or two, while Gilkenny continued to stare at the plunger, a look of longing on his face.

Barrabas said, "Let's go down, Thomas."

Gilkenny at last looked at Barrabas. At that moment Barrabas thought he saw something change in the man's eyes. A spark of life had seemed to ignite and his face become less expressionless.

"Get out of here, Nile," Gilkenny said.

"Thomas—"

"Go on, before I change my mind. Go!"

Barrabas took a step toward the man. Gilkenny edged back, so that the heel of one foot was extended over the brink.

"Don't come near me, Nile," he said. "I'll jump, or I'll throw myself on the plunger and we'll both go. Just get out of here!" he shouted.

Barrabas had exhausted all the arguments he could possibly make to convince Gilkenny he should abandon his hazardous perch and go back down the hill. And there was no way he could force down the desperate man.

"I'll go, Thomas," he said, "and I'll wait for you. You take your time and make the right decision."

"The right decision," Gilkenny repeated, his inflection toneless.

Barrabas stepped back, and risked a look behind him so that he wouldn't trip on the irregular terrain. He found the proper purchase and took one step backward off the flat top. Gilkenny was not even watching him. The P-38 hung from his hand, and he continued to stare at the plunger.

Seeing the wreck of this man who had once been a vital intrepid warrior made Barrabas sad. Despite his kidnapping, imprisonment, the involvement of all the SOBs, he felt no desire for revenge on Gilkenny.

Barrabas began to descend, and met Billy Two along the way.

Billy Two remarked, "There haven't been any shots from any direction for a while."

"Maybe it's over down there," Barrabas said. "I know it's over up here."

"THERE!" O'Toole had spotted the two men who were shooting at something below them—probably Nanos and Hayes. One stopped to reload, and as he did so, he looked up and saw O'Toole, with Hatton close behind him.

"Muller!" the man shouted. He tried to bring his weapon to bear on O'Toole, but the Irishman squeezed his trigger first and the man went down beneath a hail of death. He'd been far enough from the other man, Muller, and O'Toole's shots had been so concentrated, that Muller escaped unharmed.

His comrade's warning had caused Muller to turn quickly. His eyes met O'Toole's. They stared at each other for several seconds. Since O'Toole had not fired, Hatton held her fire, as well, watching the two men.

"You're the last one, Muller," O'Toole said. "There's no point in dying now."

"Fighting to the death is what I get paid for. It's what we all get paid for, and our job isn't finished until we do it."

O'Toole shook his head. "That's not the way I look at it."

"That's the only way *to* look at it," Muller said grimly. His finger tightened on the trigger.

WHEN THE FIRING from above had stopped, Nanos and Hayes ran, wondering how far they'd get before the second man resumed the assault. They ran ten feet, twenty feet, then stopped abruptly. No shots had been fired. They turned and looked at each other.

"What the hell?" Nanos said.

GILKENNY STARED at the plunger, then knelt down next to it. He laid the gun down on the hot stone floor, burning his hand at the same time. He pulled his hand quickly away from the source of the pain, lifting his fingers to his mouth. At that moment he felt like a trout in a skillet. He decided to follow Barrabas down the hill, to reconsider his plans in some cooler place.

His fingers went to the connection on the plunger, and he began to unscrew the wires.

That was when the plastic explosive—old, unstable stuff Gilkenny had bought from Stan Wolenski, which had been exposed for hours to the insistent heat of the sun—reached the flash point and blew.

The explosion rocked the ground under the feet of Billy Two and Barrabas

"Head for cover!" Barrabas shouted. Chunks of rock hailed down on them as they dived for what little shelter they could find on the barren rocky hillside.

O'TOOLE SAW that Muller was about to fire. His own finger had begun to tighten on the trigger—when the explosion came.

He turned. Muller looked up, as well. The peak from which Gilkenny had been watching them exploded, rocks and smoke spouting from it. The very ground where O'Toole and Muller stood shifted under their feet. It was as if the column of stone was a cannon, and the cannon had been fired.

O'Toole shouted to Hatton, "Cover!"

Hatton hit the deck. O'Toole dived toward her, partly covered her body with his own, aware that while he might have aggravated her wound, he might also have saved her life.

Bits of stone rained down on them—the smaller pieces that had been thrown the farthest from the point of detonation.

Down below, Nanos and Hayes heard the explosion and felt the ground shake, but from their position they had no idea what was happening.

Hayes looked at Nanos and said, "What the fuck!"

Then they both jumped back as a man's body just missed hitting them.

15

Barrabas listened to Erika's steady breathing as she lay beside him. It was the fourth night since his return. The SOBs and Jessup had scattered, going back to their everyday lives until some emergency called them again. Barrabas's gratitude had been unspoken, but eloquently expressed in looks. They all understood how much he appreciated their friendship, their loyalty, their risking their lives to save his.

He rose from the bed without waking Erika and went to stand naked on the balcony.

Down there somewhere a woman named Julianne had gone back to her life. When they had reached Athens she offered to give Barrabas what she had promised. Longing only to return to Erika, he had turned her down. When he asked her what she would do now, she'd shrugged, but he knew she would go back to her pimp, or another pimp. What else was there for her to do?

Barrabas had not even heard the full story of what the SOBs had gone through to find him. It wasn't important. All that *was* important was that they had come and they had found him. He didn't know about Stanley Wolenski, or Socrates Stanapolous, or Demetrius

Kontiza, or any of the other people the SOBs had encountered—or killed—during their search.

He did know about the men Gilkenny had assembled. He knew that the last one, Muller, had fallen over a ledge when the explosion had thrown him off balance, and that with that fall they were all dead. He was sorry for that. They had been soldiers working for a madman, working for hire, which was basically just what he and the SOBs did, too.

He thought about Gilkenny, and the change he had seen in the man's eyes, before he ordered Barrabas to withdraw. He wondered if Gilkenny had depressed the plunger, or if the sun had finally triggered the unstable plastic.

He liked to think that maybe in that last moment the man had regained his sanity, and perhaps had been on his way down when the peak blew up.

Or would it be better to think that, in his madness, he had done himself in? It would have been terrible to regain one's sanity and then have to face death the very next moment.

Barrabas had had enough of Greece. In the morning he and Erika were leaving for Amsterdam. They would see her brother, Gunther, there.

He was still standing on the balcony, enjoying the play of the night breeze over his skin, when he heard Erika's voice from behind him.

"Nile!"

There was fear in her voice, as if she were afraid that she had only dreamed he had come back to her.

"I'm here," he said, turning toward the door into the bedroom. "I'm coming, Erika."

Phoenix Force—bonded in secrecy to avenge the acts of terrorists everywhere.

Super Phoenix Force #2

American "killer" mercenaries are involved in a KGB plot to overthrow the government of a South Pacific island. The American President, anxious to preserve his country's image and not disturb the precarious position of the island nation's government, sends in the experts—Phoenix Force—to prevent a coup.

A stark account of one of the Vietnam War's most controversial
defense actions.

VIETNAM: GROUND ZERO™

Shifting
FIRES

ERIC HELM

For seventy-seven days and nights six thousand Marines held the
remote plateau of Khe Sanh without adequate supplies or am-
munition. As General Giap's twenty thousand troops move in to
bring the NVA one step closer to victory, an American Special
Forces squad makes a perilous jump into the mountainous Khe
Sanh territory in a desperate attempt to locate and destroy Giap's
command station.

Mack Bolan's

by Dick Stivers

Action writhes in the reader's own streets as Able Team's Carl "Ironman" Lyons, Pol Blancanales and Gadgets Schwarz make triple trouble in blazing war. Join Dick Stivers's Able Team as it returns to the United States to become the country's finest tactical neutralization squad in an era of urban terror and unbridled crime.

"Able Team will go anywhere, do anything, in order to complete their mission. Plenty of action! Recommended!"
—*West Coast Review of Books*

Able Team titles are available wherever paperbacks are sold.

AT-1

Mack Bolan's

PHOENIX FORCE

by Gar Wilson

The battle-hardened, five-man commando unit known as Phoenix Force continues its onslaught against the hard realities of global terrorism in an endless crusade for freedom, justice and the rights of the individual. Schooled in guerrilla warfare, equipped with the latest in lethal weapons, Phoenix Force's adventures have made them a legend in their own time. Phoenix Force is the free world's foreign legion!

"Gar Wilson is excellent! Raw action attacks the reader on every page."

—Don Pendleton

Phoenix Force titles are available wherever paperbacks are sold.

PF-1

TAKE 'EM NOW

FOLDING SUNGLASSES
FROM GOLD EAGLE

Mean up your act with these tough, street-smart shades. Practical, too, because they fold 3 times into a handy, zip-up polyurethane pouch that fits neatly into your pocket. Rugged metal frame. Scratch-resistant acrylic lenses. Best of all, they can be yours for only $6.99.

MAIL YOUR ORDER TODAY.

Send your name, address, and zip code, along with a check or money order for just $6.99 + .75¢ for postage and handling (for a total of $7.74) payable to Gold Eagle Reader Service. (New York and Iowa residents please add applicable sales tax.)

Remove from pouch...

unfold once...

unfold twice...

and they're ready to wear.

GOLD EAGLE

Gold Eagle Reader Service
901 Fuhrmann Blvd.
P.O. Box 1396
Buffalo, N.Y. 14240-1396

GES-1A

Offer not available in Canada.